inspired by the true story of Hope

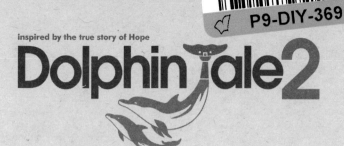

Dolphin Tale 2

inspired by the true story of Hope

Dolphin Tale 2

Dolphin Tale 2:
The Junior Novel

Adapted by Gabrielle Reyes

Based upon the screenplay written by
Charles Martin Smith

SCHOLASTIC INC.

ISBN 978-0-545-68174-2

10 9 8 7 6 5 4 3 2   14 15 16 17 18 19/0
Printed in the U.S.A.   40
First printing, August 2014

CHAPTER ONE

SPLASH! Mandy waded into the water and giggled as a school of tiny silvery fish darted past her feet.

"It's squishy!" she called to her older brother, wiggling her toes in the wet sand. "There's little fish, Troy. Come see!"

Troy stood on the beach and saw his six-year-old sister swinging a bucket in the distance. She had wandered past the end of the beach and was up to her knees in a muddy lagoon. "Mandy!" he shouted. "You better come back. Mom's gonna be mad!"

Mandy ignored her brother and followed the little fish swimming around a bend. Troy hurried down the beach. He was two years older and knew his mom expected him to watch out for his little sister. If anything happened to her, he'd be in big trouble. When Troy got to the end of the beach, he trudged through the muddy shallows, annoyed. He reached down and scooped up a handful of mud to throw at his sister. Just as he was about to toss it, he heard Mandy gasp and drop her bucket. Mandy's eyes grew wide and her mouth stood agape. *What now?* he thought. He followed the direction of her stare and couldn't believe what he saw.

A huge bottlenose dolphin was staring back at them.

* * *

Kyle Connellan gripped the steering wheel as the Clearwater Marine Aquarium's truck bounced up and down on the Florida dirt road. He had to get the team to the lagoon—and fast. Within moments, the truck lurched to a stop and the aquarium's emergency staff scrambled out. Kyle jumped out of the driver's side with ease. It had been several years since he injured his leg in the army. Watching him move, no one would ever guess that he needed a brace to help him walk. He ran his hand along the side of the truck with CMA's logo and tagline, Rescue-Rehabilitate-Release, then opened the back door. Marine mammal specialists Phoebe, Kat, and Rebecca, and his cousin Sawyer, immediately started to load the stretcher with wet towels. Kyle took a second to look at his fifteen-year-old cousin, Sawyer. He could still remember a time when Sawyer felt awkward and shy talking to anyone other than him and didn't know a thing about marine animals. It was only four years ago that Sawyer had found Winter, a wild dolphin with her tail caught in a crab trap. The few months after that had been life changing—for Sawyer and the dolphin. Winter's tail was so badly injured that it had to be amputated. Without her tail, she could only swim by moving the back of her body from side to side. But since dolphins aren't built to swim that way, this caused major damage to her spine. The doctors didn't think she would make it. If it hadn't been for Sawyer's crazy idea to ask the doctor who made Kyle's leg brace to make a prosthetic tail for Winter, the dolphin wouldn't have survived. It turned out that working with Winter and the other CMA staff, like the head of the animal hospital, Dr. Clay Haskett, and his daughter, Hazel, helped Sawyer get over his shyness and made him excited about something for the first time in his life. Winter was able to save Sawyer just as much as he saved her. And here Sawyer was rescuing a dolphin again. But this time, he was confident, happy, and part of the CMA staff. *I am the youngest CMA staff member*, Sawyer thought. *Well . . . except for Hazel.*

* * *

"When CMA staff arrived on scene, CMA 1307A was found struggling on her left side," Sawyer narrated. On the television, video footage played of Kyle,

Phoebe, Kat, Rebecca, and Sawyer running past Mandy, Troy, and their mom at the lagoon. "Her blowhole was largely submerged. She had small lesions, mucus coming out of her eyes, and was severely sunburned, a common problem with beached dolphins, as their skin isn't adapted for prolonged exposure to the sun." Sawyer looked around at the room of new CMA volunteers. He felt a little weird listening to his own voice describing the latest dolphin rescue over Hazel's video footage.

"The team suspected possible lung infection," Sawyer-the-narrator continued as the video showed the staff trying to lift the dolphin's blowhole out of the water. "Which led to her being disoriented . . . which led to her beaching." On-screen, the dolphin flailed and knocked Kat back into the muddy water. "This dolphin was named Mandy after the little girl who found her," Sawyer said as the camera focused in on Mandy, Troy, and their mother. "Now, science doesn't know whether dolphins feel emotion the way we do—fear, joy, sadness. But their brains are as complex as ours—and to us, Mandy seemed terrified."

Sawyer remembered how the team worked together to gently move Mandy onto the stretcher. He heard himself describing it. "It wasn't easy, as the area was a mud flat. Mandy was eight and a half feet long and weighed about three hundred fifty pounds."

Sawyer focused on watching the video and tried to ignore his voice-overs. He watched as he, Phoebe, and Kat gave Mandy fluids and antibiotics for her respiratory infection back at the aquarium, followed by Dr. Clay and Clay's father, Reed, spreading a topical ointment on her sunburn. Sawyer couldn't help but smile as the screen showed later footage of Mandy swimming in the medical pool. "Since then, she's been gaining strength every day and is well on the road back to being a healthy animal," he heard himself conclude.

The room of volunteers applauded as the film credits filled the screen. *Directed by Hazel Haskett. Cinematography by Hazel Haskett. Edited by Hazel Haskett. Hazel-H Productions. All rights reserved.*

"All right, everyone," Sawyer said, addressing

the volunteers. "Next session, we'll go into more detail about *strandings*, marine animals that get stuck in shallow water or on beaches. Before we go, I just want to thank all of you for volunteering. You guys are what keeps CMA going. . . ." He shrugged. "You . . . and really big truckloads of fish." He smiled as the volunteers laughed. "See you all Wednesday."

Sawyer was gathering his papers and getting ready to leave when two girls around his age approached him.

"Hi . . . uh . . . Sawyer . . . ?" said a girl with dark, straight hair.

Sawyer looked up, startled.

"Sorry—we just wanted to say thanks," said the girl, stumbling over her words. "The reason we volunteered was 'cause we heard all about you and Winter—"

"All Susie ever talks about is dolphins," her friend said, jumping in. "She wants to be just like you."

Susie felt her cheeks get hot. "I do not."

The three were standing together awkwardly when Hazel poked her head in the door. "Sawyer, we're ready to—" She paused when she saw the two starstruck girls, who looked maybe a year older than her. "We're ready to start," she said, looking back at Sawyer casually.

"Oh. Right." Sawyer glanced from Hazel to the girls. "Excuse me . . ." he said, shifting his papers. With a slight blush, he headed out the door.

CHAPTER TWO

"**E**ek!" cried a woman as her bag fell to the ground with a thud. Huge crowds of tourists were bustling through the Great Hall of the Clearwater Marine Aquarium. After Winter's success with the prosthetic tail, the former marine animal hospital had been renovated and expanded to become a first-class aquarium. Hundreds of visitors flooded the halls every day to see the exhibits and the star dolphin. The Great Hall was filled with people standing in line to buy tickets for the movies about rescued animals, school groups exploring the marine life exhibits, and patrons studying the maps, planning out their day. With all the distractions, someone was using the opportunity to try to steal a bag! The woman whipped around to stop the thief and saw it was . . . a pelican?!

"Rufus! No!" Rebecca came rushing over. But Rufus was too fast. With his big beak, he snatched a teddy bear that had fallen out of the bag and ran off, disappearing into the crowd.

"My bear!"

"Oh!" Rebecca looked down and noticed a little girl pointing after Rufus and clinging to the leg of the woman who had dropped the bag. "I am so sorry—"

"If you can't control your pelican, you shouldn't have him here!" said the toddler's mother.

"Rufus isn't exactly *our* pelican. . . ." Rebecca replied. Hazel had named him Rufus a long time ago because he lived on the roof of the aquarium. He came and went as he pleased.

"Well, whose pelican is he, then?" asked the woman, getting more and more irritated.

Rebecca thought for a moment. "I—I don't think he really belongs to anybody. . . ." She looked back down at the young girl and had an idea. "Why don't we go to the gift shop? Pick out something new?" When the little girl nodded, Rebecca led her and her mother toward the gift shop. *That Rufus* . . . she thought. *Always getting in trouble* . . .

* * *

Over at the aquarium's outdoor rooftop dolphin pools, Hazel adjusted the microphone and looked out at the crowd on the bleachers. "Ladies and gentlemen," she began. "Please give a warm welcome to champion surfer Bethany Hamilton!" The audience applauded enthusiastically. They couldn't wait to watch Bethany meet Winter. Bethany Hamilton had not only placed first in national championships, she had done it after losing her arm in a shark attack when she was just thirteen years old. Now in her twenties, Bethany continued to surf professionally.

As Bethany took the stage, Sawyer stood on a platform over the East Pool, which was holding Winter and Panama, the aquarium's one other female dolphin. He held out a yellow rubber-duck ring. It was a signal to Winter to come up and get her prosthetic tail. Winter scooted up to the platform and made a trilling sound that resembled a tweeting bird. She used it to communicate with Sawyer ever since he rescued her. Then she pushed her rostrum, the beak-like part of her face, through the ring.

"Thanks, everyone," Bethany said, taking the mic from Hazel. "It's such an honor and a blessing to be here with you, so we can show our appreciation for the wonderful work being done here at Clearwater Marine Aquarium." She looked over at Sawyer petting Winter. "Winter is a remarkable dolphin who's been such an inspiration to me and, I know, to all of you, too."

As if on cue, Winter sent a splash of water into Sawyer's face, making the crowd laugh. Sawyer groaned and wiped his face. Then he stepped aside to make room for Bethany on the platform.

"Winter normally does two sessions a day with her prosthetic, and as you can see, she really likes it," Hazel explained, having taken the mic back from Bethany. She gestured to Phoebe and Sawyer, who were now showing the surfer how to attach the plastic tail to Winter. "With it on, she can swim normally—using up- and downstrokes—and already it's stopped the damage to her spine. She's living a healthy, happy—"

Winter interrupted by splashing Sawyer in the face again.

"—life," Hazel said with a smile.

"Cut it out, Winter," Sawyer whispered. He turned to Bethany. "Just hold the tail out where she can see it."

Bethany lifted the tail and tilted it toward Winter. But instead of staying still, Winter wiggled restlessly. She looked at Sawyer and tweeted, then squirmed to look over at the other dolphin swimming in the pool.

"Looks like Winter is being extra playful today," Hazel joked.

Sawyer muttered under his breath, "She's being a brat."

Bethany looked worried. "Maybe it's me."

"No, no," Sawyer said, watching Winter. "She loves people. She's just in a weird mood for some reason."

"Winter loves the tail, but she's still young, like a teenager in human terms. And you know how we teenagers can be," Hazel said, entertaining the audience like a pro.

Everyone laughed except the dolphin trainers. Phoebe eyed Winter and the other dolphin, Panama, still swimming in the pool. "Can you gate Panama?" Phoebe called to another trainer. "I think she's distracting Winter."

As the other trainer signaled Panama to swim over to a connected pool, then closed the gate, Hazel continued. "That was Panama. She was rescued twelve years ago. She couldn't catch her own fish, and we found out why—she's deaf. Even though she's much older than Winter—she's over forty, we think—she and Winter are best friends."

Winter seemed calmer once Panama was gated, and Sawyer was able to pet her while Phoebe showed Bethany how to attach her tail. "Okay, Winter. Good girl," said Phoebe, guiding Winter back into the water. The dolphin slid off the platform and into the pool. She swam gracefully, moving her tail up and down.

Sawyer glanced at Bethany. "You ready?" he asked. Bethany nodded and they both dipped into the pool. Winter immediately swam up to Bethany, curious about this new person in the pool. She dipped under the surface and sent out a call. Winter listened to the echoes to learn more about her. By echolocating, she figured out that Bethany was missing an arm. Sawyer held out his hand and gestured for Bethany to do the same. When she did, Winter pushed her rostrum into the palm of Bethany's hand, making her twirl. Bethany and the crowd were delighted.

"She's amazing," Bethany said in awe.

"She likes you, Bethany!" someone called out from the crowd.

Winter made her tweeting sound.

When Winter began to swim around again, Sawyer showed Bethany how to hold Winter's top dorsal fin. Bethany took hold and Winter started to swim away, pulling Bethany behind her in a big circle. Together they glided around the pool, captivating the crowd.

* * *

Later, after Bethany and the crowds had left, Sawyer and Phoebe finished up with Winter in the pool. Sawyer removed the dolphin's tail and handed it to Phoebe. "Okay, Winter," Sawyer said. "I gotta go." Winter responded with her Tweety Bird sound. "See you tomorrow," Sawyer said, getting ready to get out. He put a blue mattress in the pool, but Winter ignored it. She tweeted louder. Sawyer was puzzled but gave a shrug. He was heading for the ladder to climb out of the pool when Winter splashed him.

"Hey!" he grumbled. Now that Winter had his attention, she bolted off the platform and swam to the gate separating her from the other pool, holding Panama.

"What is she doing?" Phoebe asked.

"I don't know. . . ." Sawyer replied. "She's acting really strange."

From by the gate, Winter whined.

Phoebe thought for a second. "Panama is, too," she added. "She didn't eat her two p.m. bucket. Or her five."

Sawyer glanced over at Panama drifting in the water. "You tell Clay?"

"Yeah, he's going to run some tests."

Sawyer and Phoebe watched in silence as Winter continued to squeal at the gate.

*　*　*

Since there was nothing they could do but wait for Panama's test results, Sawyer headed home. He pedaled his bike up the driveway and hopped off in front of his house. "Hey, Mom, I'm—" he called while walking through the front door. He stopped in surprise. His mom, Lorraine, wasn't preparing dinner as usual, but instead was sitting with two unexpected guests: his cousin Kyle and an older man with dark brown hair whom he didn't recognize.

"Sawyer, say hello to Dr. Martin Aslan," his mother said.

"Uh, hi," Sawyer said. He put his backpack down. "Nice to meet you." Sawyer looked over to his cousin and smiled slightly. "Hey, Kyle."

Sawyer took a seat and waited to see what was going on.

"Sawyer, I watched you today with Winter," Dr. Aslan began. "And everything Kyle tells me seems to be true. You really have quite a knack with dolphins."

"Dr. Aslan's my advisor at Boston University," Kyle explained. "He's helping me get into med school."

Sawyer nodded. "Okay . . ." *But what is Dr. Aslan*

doing here? thought Sawyer. *At my house?*

Dr. Aslan opened his briefcase and took out some brochures. "I'll get right to the point, Sawyer. We have a special program at the university for marine biology students. It's called SEA Semester. Twelve weeks on a sailing ship, a full learning experience right on the ocean." He handed the brochures to Sawyer.

Glossy photographs of dolphins and whales leapt off the page. Teenagers posed together looking goofy but happy on the deck of a majestic ship. Sawyer stared, speechless.

"Next semester, we're emphasizing marine mammals—our students get hands-on teaching from some of the finest scientific minds in the country. Sailing on a tall ship, cruising through the Caribbean. And swimming with wild dolphins in some of the most beautiful waters on earth." Dr. Aslan couldn't help but grin, seeing Sawyer entranced. He had opened the brochure to see the SEA students in scuba gear swimming inches away from schools of tropical fish, coral reefs, and a pod of hundreds of dolphins.

Dr. Aslan resumed. "Every year we invite one gifted high school student to join us. And this year . . ." Kyle and Lorraine glanced at each other and smiled. "This year, we'd like it to be you."

Sawyer's eyebrows shot up and his jaw dropped. *Did he just hear that Dr. Aslan wanted* him? As Kyle's advisor went on to explain how rigorous and challenging the program's curriculum would be, Sawyer could barely keep up. But Dr. Aslan's last words brought him out of his stupor.

"Yes, Sawyer." Dr. Aslan stopped for a moment, seeing Sawyer's incredulous look. "Full scholarship. All paid for."

Lorraine and Kyle beamed at him.

"We'll speak to your school and get you credit for the entire semester," said Dr. Aslan, shaking Sawyer's hand. "Just come to Boston with Kyle at the beginning of the term . . . and we'll take care of the rest."

CHAPTER THREE

The next morning, Sawyer biked to CMA faster than usual, as if the SEA Semester brochures sticking out of his back pocket were powering the pedals. He replayed Dr. Aslan's words from the night before. He had said that Sawyer's work with Winter was already well-known in the field. Sawyer was astounded that top marine biologists knew anything about him! He couldn't wait to tell Dr. Clay and Hazel. If it weren't for Hazel sneaking him in to see Winter after the CMA team first brought the animal to the hospital and her father, Clay, letting him help with Winter's recovery, who knows how Sawyer would be doing in school? When he found Winter, he had been on his way to summer school after failing every subject except Shop. And now here he was with a full scholarship to a once-in-a-lifetime semester abroad. He hurried through the door to find them and immediately crashed into a throng of people heading down the stairs from the upper deck. He saw Rebecca ushering guests down the stairs and hurried over to find out what was happening.

"I'm sorry, we've had an emergency. That's all I can say right now. But your ticket is good for admission anytime in the future," Rebecca explained to the visitors with an edge in her voice.

"Rebecca!" Sawyer was starting to panic. "What's going on?"

A lump filled Rebecca's throat. She couldn't break the news to Sawyer. "You better talk to Clay."

Sawyer dashed upstairs and ran onto the deck by the rooftop pools. His stomach dropped when he saw the ropes cordoning off the area by the Main

Pool. A volunteer let him pass through and Sawyer slowly approached Dr. Clay and the other staff and volunteers at the poolside. "Dr. Clay—?" Sawyer started. He stopped when he noticed Kat sobbing into the shoulder of one of the staff members. *What's wrong?* Sawyer's eyes trailed over to the pool and he gasped. Two divers were moving the body of Panama onto a stretcher.

"What . . . what happened?" Sawyer stammered.

"We don't know," Clay said, shaking his head. "She took a last breath and went down to the bottom of the pool. Kat was here . . . but there was nothing she could do."

Sawyer felt numb with shock, but when he heard a moaning sound, he jumped.

"Winter!" he exclaimed, rushing over to the East Pool.

"She was already gated when it happened. We needed Panama to be alone to run some tests," Dr. Clay went on. Even though Sawyer was right in front of him, he seemed to be talking to himself.

"She was just so old—it could have been anything."

Sawyer kneeled down and reached out to Winter, but she pulled away. As the divers lifted the stretcher with Panama on it out of the water, Winter just wanted to be alone.

* * *

Along the marina, Rufus hovered overhead against a cloudy sky. He swooped down and landed next to Sawyer, who was walking on the dock. Sawyer turned toward the houseboat, but paused when he heard crying. He looked up to the boat's crow's nest. It was Hazel. Sawyer took a deep breath, boarded the boat, and began to climb the old rope ladder.

"Hey," he said, reaching the top.

"Oh. Hey," Hazel said, wiping her eyes. "Come in. Or up. Or whatever."

Sawyer took a quick look around and stepped into the crow's nest. He hadn't been up here in a while and it looked like neither had Hazel. He remembered how much time she used to spend up here. It was like her own little tree fort at the top of the houseboat's mast. "Thanks. How you doing?" Sawyer asked gently.

Hazel shrugged. Her eyes followed Rufus, who was now flying up to the wall of the aquarium. "Why do things like this have to happen?" she asked.

"I wish I knew," Sawyer said, staring out in the distance.

"I loved Panama. I'm going to miss her so, so much." Hazel sighed. "I know she was old, but . . ."

"Yeah, but she was just—good, you know? Gentle."

A light rain started to fall but Sawyer and Hazel didn't even notice. "Dad's talked about it. He's afraid Winter might get depressed and stop doing anything. Even eating."

Sawyer nodded slowly. "That happens sometimes with dolphins."

"Can you sit with me for a bit?" Hazel asked. "Let's not talk, okay? Just sit."

Sawyer took a seat next to Hazel on the crow's nest floor. "Sure." The two sat in the misty rain watching Rufus.

* * *

Later that night, when the rain had stopped, Clay sat by the rooftop pools playing his saxophone. He wanted to keep Winter company and thought the music might cheer her up. Clay stopped and gazed into the pool, hoping to see Winter swimming at the surface. But she wouldn't come out. He could see her hiding under the platform.

Sawyer walked past Clay with a basket of pool toys and crouched down by the water. He felt a wad of wet papers sticking out of his jeans. He reached into his back pocket, grabbed the soggy SEA Semester brochures, and tossed them onto the deck. Then he pulled the yellow rubber-duck ring from the basket and held it out over the water, trying to get Winter to come out.

"How's our girl?" Clay asked.

Sawyer sighed and put down the ring. "Just staying under the platform."

Clay nodded and moved next to Sawyer.

"Do you think she knew Panama was dying?" Sawyer asked.

Clay was thoughtful. "Hard to say. Echolocation is an amazing thing. She might have seen something inside Panama that we couldn't. Maybe she was trying to tell us. When the necropsy is done, we'll have a better idea." He looked at Sawyer. "It's good you're keeping her company."

"I think she liked your saxophone playing."

Clay smiled. "Which proves she's not a music critic. Hey"—Clay picked up the wet brochures—"what's this?"

"Oh. Yeah."

Clay turned the pages of the brochures. "I know this program. It's out of Boston, right?"

Sawyer nodded. "They invited me."

"Whoa. Really? Sawyer, that's very cool."

"Kyle put my name in. They're giving me a scholarship."

Clay raised his eyebrows, impressed. "That's fantastic, buddy! This is a big deal. When do you go?"

Sawyer shrugged. "September something," he mumbled. "But it's for three months. You think it's okay for me to leave Winter that long?"

"She'll be fine."

"But we have to pair her with another female, don't we?" Sawyer knew that because dolphins are such social animals, a law required them to live with at least one other.

"Yes, that's the law. And it's a good one."

Sawyer was tentative. "We've got Mandy now. . . ."

"Yes, we do," Clay replied carefully. "And you know what they say—when one door shuts, another opens. But let's get through this one day at a time."

A moment later, Winter came out from under the platform and swam to the surface to take a breath. Sawyer nodded as she retreated back under the water.

CHAPTER FOUR

The CMA board of directors stared at Clay across the big conference room table. Years ago, Clay didn't enjoy meetings with the board of directors. But ever since the real estate developer Phil Hordern had bought CMA, he had not only alleviated its financial problems, he had invested in its amazing expansion. The recent board meetings had been full of exciting updates. Now Clay shifted in his seat, hating to be the bearer of bad news.

"So . . ." Patricia, one of the board members, probed. "Winter is basically depressed?"

"In dolphin terms, yes," said Clay. He consulted his notes. "Lethargic. Not interacting. Refusing food for the most part. We're increasing supplements."

"And the prosthetic?" Jackie, another board member, inquired.

"Refusing that, too."

"So it's possible that her spine is deteriorating again?" Patricia asked.

"Possible," said Clay. "I have an ultrasound and X-ray set scheduled for Friday."

Phil Hordern leaned into the table and looked directly at Clay. "It's been three weeks. During which time, you've kept the public away from her."

Clay held his gaze. "Yes. I have."

"It sounds like she's missing Panama," Jackie noted.

"But isn't it against USDA regulations? To keep a dolphin alone in a pool?" asked Patricia.

"It is," said Clay.

Patricia was puzzled. The hospital had just recently rescued a young female dolphin. "Why don't we just put Mandy in with her? Wouldn't that solve everything?"

Clay was guarded. "I can't give you an answer on that right now."

The board members exchanged a look. *Why is Clay being so difficult?*

No progress was made during the rest of the meeting. Afterward, Phil held Clay back to talk to him. "We're more than a hospital now, Clay. We're a full-blown aquarium. People come from all over the world to see, to learn—"

"I'm aware," Clay said.

"And how many of those people come to see Winter?"

"I have a medical obligation, Phil." Clay didn't like the situation any more than Phil and the rest of the board, but he had additional concerns.

"And we're meeting it, Clay. But you've seen the faces of the children, the veterans—how moved they are. Isn't that part of our mission, too?"

Clay was getting frustrated. "But you can't just

throw two dolphins into the water together! It doesn't work that way. These are intelligent, sophisticated creatures. If they don't get along, there's not a thing on God's green earth we can do about it."

Phil sighed. "Clay. I'm not telling you how to do your job. But I just think that putting Mandy in with Winter—and soon—would be one heck of a good idea."

* * *

Back at the medical pools, Hazel went to check on Mandy. "How's she doing?" she asked Phoebe and Sawyer.

"Comin' along," Phoebe said, continuing to rub lotion on Mandy's back. "Sunburn's a lot better."

Squawk! Rufus landed on the wall, flapping his wings dramatically.

"What's with Rufus?" Hazel asked, eyeing the big bird.

Sawyer shrugged. *That bird is always acting nuts,* he thought. "I don't know. He's been doing that for a couple of days. Back and forth. I think he's losing his mind."

"Not that there's much to lose."

Rufus gave Hazel a pointed look, then flew back down to the dock. *Aaaaark!* he cried.

Sawyer and Hazel looked back at each other, puzzled. "Let's go find Rebecca and check it out," Hazel proposed.

A few minutes later, Hazel, Rebecca, and Sawyer hurried over to Rufus on the corner of the dock.

"Okay, quiet now," Rebecca instructed. "We don't want to spook him."

Aaaaark! Rufus responded. He leaned over the edge of the dock and looked into the water at a small splash of movement.

The group leaned out to peer underneath the dock. "What—what's that?" asked Sawyer, craning his neck.

Hazel kneeled down and reached both of her hands under the dock. "Oh! Oh my gosh!" Hazel exclaimed, pulling out a struggling green sea turtle snarled in fishing line.

Rebecca reached down to help. "Poor thing. How long has she been under there?"

Hazel fingered the fishing hook attached to the line that was wrapped tightly around the turtle and cutting into her front flippers. "Well, at least she didn't swallow the hook."

Up in the operating room a short while later, Rebecca took charge of examining the turtle. "Lacerations aren't too bad, I guess," she said, untangling the last bit of fishing line and placing it in a pile on the exam table. "Saline."

Sawyer picked up a syringe and squirted the solution on the cuts.

"These fishermen threw old line in the water. They just don't realize. . . . Hazel . . ."

Without another word, Hazel handed over a tube of ointment.

Rebecca took the tube, squeezed out some ointment, and spread it on the turtle's wounds. "We'll need X-rays to make sure nothing's broken."

Sawyer looked up. "CT scan?"

"And blood work?" Hazel added. "Check her glucose. If she's lost blood, her iron will be low."

Rebecca smiled. *These kids know their stuff,* she thought.

Before she could answer, the group heard a loud bang at the window. They looked up. Rufus had smacked against the window and was now peering in, flapping his wings wildly.

"What on earth is wrong with that bird?" Rebecca wondered.

Hazel shook her head. "Where do I start?"

After an hour, Rebecca was lowering the turtle into one of the smaller pools in the aquarium's new turtle area. The three watched as it paddled around, exploring the new environment. "What do you think? What shall we call her?" she asked her assistants.

Hazel was thoughtful. "Mavis," she declared.

Sawyer and Rebecca looked at her with scrunched eyebrows.

"From *The Andy Griffith Show,*" she explained.

"Don't you watch any TV from *this* century?" Sawyer asked.

RAWP! Rufus was back. He perched on the wall above the pools, fluffed his feathers, and settled in.

"Great," Hazel said, rolling her eyes. "Now he's a bodyguard."

* * *

"No, I do NOT have a ticket! Nor do I intend to BUY one!"

The aquarium's teenage volunteers looked at the ornery old man wheeling a metal case behind him and froze. The surly patron had walked into the aquarium and pushed his way past the ticket booth without stopping, causing the crowds in line to grumble. "But . . . but, sir—" a volunteer stammered, holding out a hand to stop him.

"Stop clawing at me!" the man said, batting the hand away. "I've got jars of peanut butter older than you."

"Sir, if you don't have a ticket, we can't—" another volunteer began.

"And keep your grubby paws off of my case. Piranhas!"

"Dr. McCarthy!" Sawyer called out. He ran up to his old friend and noticed his familiar metal case. Sawyer realized the doctor must be there to measure Winter for a new tail. Dr. McCarthy was an expert at designing and fitting prosthetic limbs. Sawyer first met him when he was fitting Kyle's leg brace. Even though it had been several years, Sawyer was still amazed that the doctor agreed to fit Winter with a prosthetic tail. As Dr. McCarthy had said back then, no one in his right mind would ever consider such a thing. But fortunately for everyone—and most of all Winter—Dr. McCarthy claimed he was never in his right mind. "I'm sorry," Sawyer went on. "We have so many new people. They didn't realize who you were."

"That much"—Dr. McCarthy paused and straightened his jacket—"is obvious."

Ten minutes later, up at the rooftop pools, Dr. McCarthy continued to be indignant. "But we have a standing appointment," he said to Dr. Clay. "Every six months."

"I'm so sorry, it completely slipped my mind," said Clay.

"Well, surely the fish has outgrown her last tail by now."

Dr. McCarthy could see Clay's reluctance to answer. "Actually . . ." Clay said, running his hand through his hair. "We don't really know." He took a deep breath and let it out slowly. Then he explained how Panama had died and how it was affecting Winter.

The doctor took a moment to process all the news. "Doesn't she come out at all?" McCarthy asked about Winter.

"Not much," said Sawyer.

Clay thought for a moment, then decided to see if they could coax Winter out from under the platform. He walked over to the winch that controlled raising and lowering the stretcher into the water and signaled for Sawyer to beckon Winter.

Sawyer crouched down on the platform and held out the yellow rubber-duck ring. "Come on, Winter. Up you go."

Winter looked up from the bottom of the pool and saw Sawyer peering down at her. She slowly drifted up to the surface.

"Don't rush her, now. . . ." Clay coached. "Nice and slow."

"Come on, Winter," Sawyer encouraged. "We gotta make another cast of your tail. You keep growing." He pet her gently as she floated at the pool edge. "It's easy. . . . Up you go. . . ."

Winter bumped the yellow ring with her rostrum, but she didn't spear it. She looked from Sawyer to Clay to Dr. McCarthy. Then she poked her rostrum through the ring and flung it away from the pool.

Clay looked concerned. "She okay?"

Sawyer continued to stroke Winter and speak softly. "I think so." He nodded to Clay, who hit the winch button. Winter flinched as the machine powered on with a metallic groan. Sawyer lowered his face next to hers. "It's gonna be okay, Winter."

Clay hit a switch and the stretcher began to descend with loud clanks and whirs. Winter looked around frantically. As soon as she saw the stretcher, she reared up and wheeled around, belting Sawyer across the face, making him tumble into the water.

"Winter!" Clay exclaimed.

Sawyer grabbed the platform edge, but before he could pull himself out, Winter came for him. With piercing high-pitched squeals, she head-butted him in the ribs, knocking him into the side of the pool.

"Get 'em apart!" Clay shouted to the staff across the pool. Phoebe dove in, dodging Winter, who was thrashing wildly. Phoebe grabbed Sawyer's arm and pulled him to the platform as others hurried to lift him out. Then Phoebe turned back to settle down Winter, but the dolphin had already plunged to the bottom of the pool and under the platform, out of sight.

Surrounded by crystal-blue waters, a group of teenagers swam through a circle of wild dolphins. A boy just a bit older than Sawyer grabbed onto one of the dolphin's dorsal fins and smiled wide as the animal took him on a spectacular underwater ride.

"Hey," Lorraine said from the doorway to Sawyer's bedroom. Sawyer paused the video he was watching on the SEA Semester website. "I thought you might have trouble scooping it yourself," said his mother, walking over and handing him a bowl of ice cream.

"Maybe later," Sawyer said, taking the ice cream and setting it aside.

His mother nodded and leaned over to check Sawyer's lip. She didn't really think he would eat the ice cream, but she needed a reason to go in and check on her son. Sawyer's lip was still swollen. His ribs had been bandaged and his wrist was in a soft cast for a sprain. After a few silent moments, Lorraine spoke gently. "Do you have any idea why Winter might have done this?"

Sawyer shrugged. "She's a wild animal. She got freaked out."

"Did Clay say how long till you can go back in with her?"

"No," Sawyer responded, his face stoic.

Lorraine considered whether she should say anything more. "You know," she started, "Dr. Aslan is going to need an answer—"

But Sawyer cut her off. "Mom. I know. When I have an answer, I'll say so." He got up and walked out of the room. Lorraine sat down as Sawyer shut his bedroom door behind him. She thought about walking out after him but knew he just needed some space. Besides, she wondered, what could she say to make any of this easier? She glanced at Sawyer's computer and saw the SEA Semester website. She pressed PLAY on the video and watched the dolphins swimming in the sea.

CHAPTER FIVE

George Hatton sat down at the table in Clay's office, adjusted his necktie, and opened his bag. He started to spread its contents out in front of him: medical files, a worn copy of the USDA regulations book, a legal pad, a can of root beer, and a pen. He held the pen and started to write a note on his legal pad, but nothing came out.

"Oh!" Clay said, walking into his office. He saw George shaking his pen vigorously. "George, I . . . This is a surprise."

"Hello, Clay," George said. "I didn't mean to startle you. Your staff let me in." He gestured to Clay with his pen. "You got a pen I can borrow?"

Clay walked to his desk slowly, reached for a pen, and handed it to the older man with dread. George worked for the U.S. Department of Agriculture and regularly visited CMA to inspect the facility and make sure it wasn't breaking any laws designed to protect the animals. *This visit is going to be a rough one. The papers George signs with that pen are not going to be good.*

"Hey, Clay," Phoebe said, popping her head in the door. "We need to—" She stopped. When she saw whom Clay was with, she went pale.

"I may be a while, Phoebe," said Clay.

"Right," she said. She nodded, sent a worried glance over to Clay, and shut the door.

After a few minutes, George packed up his files and the two men left Clay's office to tour the building. They started at the rooftop pools.

"So, is the necropsy on CMA 0219 in yet?" he asked, referring to Panama.

"No. It'll be another month," said Clay.

"Preliminary results?" asked George.

"Well, she was confirmed at forty years old, and the pathology does point to respiratory failure."

George nodded. "Pretty common at that age. And her companion?" He looked at his notes. "CMA 1108?"

"Winter?" Clay gestured toward the pools. "Over here." Clay walked with George into the cordoned-off area and past the sign that read "We're sorry, Winter is unavailable to the public until further notice."

When they reached the edge of the East Pool, George pulled out his medical files. "Behavior's off," he said, reading. "Elevated cortisol levels . . ." He peered at Winter. "Clay—this animal is stressed."

"I know. We're doing routine medical workups and keeping a twenty-four-hour watch."

George made a note. Then he looked up and gave Clay a pointed look. *Clay is a smart guy. He has to know what's coming.* "And you're aware—it's a major violation for her to be isolated like this."

Clay had imagined this conversation over and over again. Still, the implications of what could happen to Winter hit him like a punch in the stomach. "It's just temporary," Clay said. "We have Mandy—uh, 1307A—who is rehabbing very well. We're hoping to pair them as soon as possible."

George scribbled more notes. "And when would that be?"

"Uh . . . I'm not sure. We don't have a date scheduled."

George eyed Clay with suspicion.

"Yet," Clay added.

"I see," George said, and wrote that in his notes, too.

*   *   *

Hours later, Clay stood at the medical pools watching Mandy play with a toy in the water. He glanced at a desk where George continued to write lengthy notes on his legal pad. Finally, the inspector looked up.

"Clay?" George straightened his papers and walked over to Clay. "I'm going to be frank with you."

Clay stood motionless. "Please do."

"I'm citing you for a number of violations," said George. He read from his notes. "Your backup generator hasn't been tested in six months. Fish freezer in the kitchen is a couple degrees high." He pointed to some bottles beside the pool. "Those chemicals aren't labeled legibly. And take a look at the wiring for your webcams, will ya?"

Clay swallowed. "Sure, of course." He hoped that was everything.

"However, the most egregious violation is your female bottlenose." George went on reading from his notes. "Winter is stressed. She's isolated. Her scoliosis is worsening." George looked at Clay once more, his expression grave. "She needs to be paired with another female ASAP. I know you know that, Clay. I'm just making it official."

Clay tightened his jaw and nodded.

George handed Clay the violation. "You have thirty days to correct the problem."

* * *

Across town in a crowded waiting room, one patient was getting a lot of attention.

"Mavis Haskett?" a nurse's aide said, reading from a clipboard. She looked up and saw everyone was staring at her next patient. *A turtle?*

"Yup!" said Hazel. "This is Mavis," she announced, holding up the turtle.

After the nurse picked her jaw up off the floor, she guided Hazel, Mavis, and Rebecca to the CT scan room, where Lorraine was setting up the machine.

"I hear you're getting your own MRI machine soon," Lorraine said, adjusting Mavis on the scanner. The turtle had to be in just the right position for the machine to capture images of her organs and bones. "I'll miss these visits." She smiled. "Now step back, Hazel." She looked at the young lady in front of her and shook her head in awe. *How are she and Sawyer growing up so fast?* she wondered. Then she turned her attention back to the turtle. "Say 'cheese,' Mavis," Lorraine said, and pushed the button.

* * *

Back at the aquarium, Susie was hesitant. Sawyer was sitting by the edge of Winter's pool and she didn't want to bother him, but she couldn't bear wasting the opportunity. She approached the pool. "Uh . . . Sawyer?" Sawyer turned around and looked at Susie blankly. "Sorry to bother you, but, uh . . ." She pointed to an elderly man behind her. "That's my grandpa."

Sawyer glanced back. Susie's grandfather was wearing a baseball cap that read "3rd Marine Division, Vietnam Veteran" and standing on a prosthetic leg covered with an American flag decal. Sawyer wasn't sure what to do, so he gave a small wave at the man, who responded with a jaunty salute.

"He's just visiting," Susie continued. "And . . . I know nobody's supposed to get close to Winter, but I was wondering if there's any chance he could just have a peek—"

"Now, Suze, don't strong-arm the man," her grandfather said.

"Grandpa, I'm not. I'm just asking." She looked at Sawyer. "If not, we totally understand."

The hope in Susie's voice hit Sawyer in the heart. He thought for a moment. "Come on," he said, getting up on his feet. He led them toward the stairs.

"Right behind you, Commander," said Susie's grandpa. His prosthetic leg clunked as the three went down the stairs. Susie offered out her arm but her grandfather shooed it away. "I've been walking on this thing since before your mom was born," he said, giving her a wink.

Sawyer led them through the crowd in the aquarium's Great Hall and down a side hall that was only accessible to staff. They entered a big room that was under renovation and that Susie had never been in before. Susie surveyed the scaffolding up against the walls, which were covered in tarps. When she realized Sawyer was already pulling some tarps away from the wall, she walked over to help him.

"Oh! What happened to your hand?" she said, noticing his cast.

Sawyer shrugged. "Oh, nothing. I fell," he mumbled.

Susie was about to ask how he fell when Sawyer lifted the last tarp, exposing a small viewing window into the East Pool.

"There you go," Sawyer said.

For a moment, Susie and her grandfather were speechless as they took in a square view of the pool from under the water's surface. Her grandfather limped up to the window and peered through the glass at Winter resting under the platform. "Well," he whispered, "will you look at that?" Susie's grandfather looked Winter in the eye, then his eyes traced along the dolphin's body. "Man," he said, taking in her stump, "there's nothin' there." He looked back to Sawyer. "How come she's not wearin' her rig?" he asked, moving one of his hands to his own prosthetic leg.

"She's been kinda down lately. She hasn't really felt like wearing it," Sawyer explained.

From the other side of the glass, Winter drifted over to the window, curious to see who was visiting her. She watched the young lady walk up to the older man and saw him put his arm around her. The man nodded. "Yeah," he said softly, "we all get that."

CHAPTER SIX

"**O**kay, Mandy. All done!" Phoebe chirped. Mandy slid off the platform and into the pool while Phoebe labeled her blood sample. The young dolphin disappeared from the water's surface only to leap out of the water a moment later. *Splish!*

"Got a lot of moxie," Reed observed from the side of the pool. He glanced at his son, Clay, standing beside him, and then continued to adjust the settings on the pool's filter system. Clay nodded. He had seen the leap, too.

"Clay? You want a full panel done on these?" Phoebe asked.

"Yeah," Clay said, watching Mandy zip around the perimeter of the pool in a circle then take a big leap out of the water. *Splash!*

"Her sunburn's a lot better," Phoebe said, following his gaze.

Clay nodded again and caught his father staring at him. They locked eyes for a second, thinking the same thing: *That's one very healthy-looking dolphin.*

* * *

The next day, Clay called Sawyer and Hazel into his office. "So . . . I've got all of Mandy's test results. And I wanted to talk to you two before I briefed anyone else." He motioned for the two teens to take a seat at the table. "The blood work all came back fine. The X-rays of her lungs look good," he said, reading from his files. "There's no sign of infection, so we've discontinued antibiotics. White cell count is normal and her sunburn's healed." He looked up at them. "Pretty much a clean bill of health."

Sawyer and Hazel exchanged looks.

"That's fantastic!" Hazel exclaimed.

"It's one of the most successful rehabs we've ever done," Clay agreed.

"So," Hazel said with a wide smile. "When can we put her in with Winter?"

Clay paused. He took a deep breath. "Hazel. What I'm saying is—Mandy is fine."

Hazel started to nod, but then a cloud came over her eyes and her face fell. She looked at Sawyer, whose face had gone pale, too.

"As you know, we have an equal obligation to every animal that—" Clay continued.

"But you can't let her go!" Sawyer burst out. "We're gonna pair her with Winter!"

Clay kept his voice steady. "If she can survive in the wild, how can I keep her?"

Hazel was horrified. "You don't have to keep her forever! Just a year—or six months—just until we find another—"

"We have no idea what's going to happen, Hazel," said her father. "We might wait two years, or five, or ten. . . . Don't you think we have to consider Mandy? Don't you think she deserves to go home if she can?"

"But we'll lose Winter!" Hazel fought through the feeling of her throat closing. "We lost Panama and now we're going to lose Mandy and then—"

"Hazel, I haven't decided yet!" Clay snapped. *Doesn't Hazel realize this isn't an easy decision for me?* After all, he cared about Winter, too. He took another deep breath. "But if Mandy can catch live fish—which you know is the last test—that is the decision I am going to have to make."

* * *

Later that night, Clay stepped out onto the deck of the houseboat and found Reed mending a shirt. "Hey," he said to his dad.

"Hey . . . How's Hazel?" Reed asked.

Clay sighed. "Gone to bed. Let's just say I'm not exactly her favorite person right now."

Reed smiled and shrugged, not looking up from his needle and thread. "Well, whaddya gonna do?"

Clay sat down next to his father and stared at the light reflecting on the surface of the water. Reed paused to look up at his son. "So, what *are* you gonna do?" he asked more gently this time.

"I don't know." Clay shot a side look at his father. "Something tells me you've got some fatherly advice all lined up, though."

"Oh, I've always got that." Reed laughed. "In this case, I only got three words for you. And they're yours, not mine."

Clay's eyebrows scrunched together. "Mine?"

"All the way back when we started this place—just after the Civil War . . ." he joked. The two men chuckled. "You wrote three words. On the back of a cocktail napkin at Frenchy's, if I remember."

Clay smiled, thinking back. "Rescue. Rehabilitate. Release."

"The words you built this place on. You didn't build it to keep animals. You built it to heal 'em and let 'em go. . . . Tell me something. Poor Winter can't ever go home. But if she could . . . ?"

"In a heartbeat."

"There you go," said Reed.

Clay regarded his father. He always seemed to know what to say. Clay had an idea. "Dad, how do I tell Hazel?"

"Beats me," said Reed with a shrug. "I got enough trouble tryin' to figure out how to talk to you."

Clay sighed. He was on his own for that one.

That night, Clay couldn't sleep. He tossed and turned all night until finally he got up at the break of dawn. He went to the kitchen to fix himself a cup of coffee and noticed something moving outside his window.

"Hazel?" he called, opening the door of the houseboat. His daughter was wearing a hoodie and shorts and lacing up her sneakers. "What are you doing, honey?"

"Going for a run," she answered without looking up from her shoes.

"I'm thinking we should talk. . . ."

"No. You're thinking *you* should talk," she shot back, "and that I should listen."

Clay felt like he had been slapped across the face. He hated when Hazel was mad at him. "Hazel, come on now—"

"I told you. I'm going for a run." Without waiting for his response, Hazel ran up the gangplank and down the marina.

"Hazel!" Clay shouted. *She wouldn't really take off like that, would she?* But when she turned down the dock and out of sight, he had his answer. Clay kicked a chair, making it topple over. Then he noticed his father in the doorway of the houseboat. He had seen the whole thing.

* * *

At first Hazel just ran. She just had to get away from the aquarium . . . and from her father. How could he even think of releasing Mandy back into the wild when they needed her in order to keep Winter? Her father said it wasn't fair to Mandy, but losing Winter wasn't fair either. Hazel's feet pounded harder against the pavement. She knew she needed to talk to someone who understood how important Winter was and who might be able to talk sense into her father. Up ahead, Hazel saw the sign for the Clearwater General Hospital and she knew what to do.

Half an hour later, Hazel and Lorraine took their coffee cups to a bench in front of the hospital. "It's like I'm a plate-glass window. He doesn't even see me," Hazel complained. "He doesn't listen to me or tell me things. All I'm saying is to keep Mandy a few months. Just until Winter's settled, and maybe we can pair her up with another female. But he won't even *try*. It's like he doesn't even care about Winter."

"Oh, you know that's not true, Hazel," said Lorraine. "But he has tough decisions to make. . . ." She trailed off as the blare of an ambulance's siren drowned out the sound of her voice. Lorraine and Hazel watched the ambulance pull up next to the emergency room. Two paramedics jumped out of

Winter playing in the pool.

Sawyer and the other aquarium volunteers love helping marine animals!

Winter made friends with surfing champion Bethany Hamilton.

Rufus pestering the visitors . . . again!

Clay tells Sawyer about Panama.

Sawyer is given an opportunity to study marine mammals with Dr. Aslan.

Sawyer, Hazel, and Rebecca examine Mavis.

Sawyer is concerned about Winter.

The team celebrates Mandy's release!

Clay rushes Hope to a pool.

Everybody has "Hope for Winter."

Sawyer and Hazel love to play with Winter in the pool.

Hazel is happy with Winter's progress.

Winter and Hope became friends!

the back and unloaded a patient on a stretcher. Next, three hospital staff members rushed the patient into the building.

"You know . . . I don't know much about dolphins, but I do know about hospitals," Lorraine said, deep in thought. "You know what I think sometimes? What if one day, I came to work—and the whole place was empty? Room after room, no patients. Just doctors, nurses, all sitting around bored because everybody in town is fine. Nobody is sick. Nobody needs surgery. Wouldn't that be great?"

Hazel tried to follow.

"These patients aren't here because they want to be," Lorraine explained. "They're here because they *need* to be. Nobody stays a single minute longer than they have to."

Hazel looked down at her coffee cup. She knew what Lorraine was getting at.

"Talk to your dad. Children grow up so fast—it's hard for parents to keep up sometimes. Just talk—the way you'd want him to talk to you." Lorraine lifted the corners of her mouth. "Do something grown-up. Take him to coffee, maybe."

Hazel scoffed. "I hate coffee. This is hot chocolate."

* * *

"You know, I was born the year you and Mom started the aquarium," Hazel declared. She had run back to the aquarium from the hospital and found her father working at Mandy's pool.

Hazel had startled Clay but he tried not to show it. "I guess that's true. . . ."

"It's not right to exclude me from things. I'm not a child. I'm as capable of making informed decisions as anyone here."

Clay nodded. *She's right.* "Yes. Yes, you are."

"If we're going to consider Mandy a candidate for release, I would like to see her files," Hazel said—just as she had practiced in her head while running on the way back. "Medical records, blood work, cytology, everything. I'd like to read them now."

Clay's eyes grew wide.

"Please," Hazel added.

Her father blinked slowly, then turned to the files stacked on the metal cart beside him. He picked them up and handed them to Hazel. *How is this the same little girl who would howl and giggle when I used to toss her in the air?*

Hazel took the files. Without another word, she went to find a quiet place to sit. She had a lot of reading to do.

* * *

That afternoon, Hazel directed the others at Mandy's pool. She had spent all morning reading the files. As much as she wanted to disagree with her father, it was clear that Mandy was fully rehabilitated. "Phoebe, are those the fish?" she asked as Phoebe brought over a large cooler.

"Yeah, a dozen," Phoebe replied.

"That should be fine." Hazel opened the cooler and took a look at the live capelin fish. She turned to Sawyer, already standing in the pool with Mandy.

"All right. We're ready. Sawyer, hold her attention."

Sawyer used a rubber toy to get Mandy's attention, then stroked her head while Hazel brought the cooler to the edge of the pool and put it down where the dolphin couldn't see it.

"When I say," said Hazel. She took a net and scooped out three squirming fish from the cooler. She quickly dumped them into the pool. Hazel, Sawyer, and Phoebe held their breath as they watched the fish scatter in the water. "Now, Sawyer," commanded Hazel.

Sawyer let go of Mandy's face and stepped away from the animal. *Whap! Whap!* In seconds, Mandy had gobbled up two fish. She spun around to chase the third—*whap!* She swallowed it in one gulp.

"Whoa," Phoebe whispered. "Good girl."

The group stood together in silence, feeling the same mix of emotions. Without a doubt, Mandy had passed the last test.

* * *

"Of *course* you have a choice!" Phil Hordern bellowed. He started pacing around the boardroom, walking back and forth past an architectural model of the expanded aquarium.

Clay started to explain the situation—again. "My obligation—"

"I'll tell you what your obligation is," Phil ranted. "It's to this institution. The people, the animals, and the work you've done for the last few years. And what about the community? Think what Winter means to them." The board director swept his arm over the model. "You're jeopardizing everything."

Clay clamped his jaw. "I founded this place on the principles of—"

"I *know* the principles. But if you let Mandy go, the government will take Winter. End of story."

"Somebody might still have a—"

"A what?" Phil interrupted. "A bottlenose? Female? That they haven't paired and that can't be released? They don't, Clay. We've tried."

"If Mandy can catch live fish, I cannot morally keep her in captivity!" Clay said finally, raising his voice.

Phil wanted to shout back but he kept his voice level. "We'll lose Winter."

Clay rubbed his forehead and took a deep breath. "We might. But when we shook hands that day on the dock, you told me I could run the place my way—and that's what I'm doing." The two men glared at each other. "And if you don't like it, fire me."

CHAPTER SEVEN

Clay watched as his staff lifted the stretcher carrying Mandy into the back of the truck. Mandy made a high-pitched chirping sound.

"Sounds like she really wants to go," Hazel said.

Clay looked at his daughter. He knew this was Hazel's way of apologizing. He put his hand on her shoulder and nodded.

"Keep her sternal!" Phoebe instructed. "Easy now . . . smooth."

"I figure you've been on enough releases," Clay said to Hazel. "Why don't you run this one?"

Hazel was stunned. *Does he really mean it?*

"Oh, come on, you could do it in your sleep," Clay joked, seeing her expression. "Just promise me you won't."

Hazel laughed just as Mandy vocalized. The dolphin was confused. *Why isn't she in the pool? What's happening?*

Kat signaled to Clay from the back of the truck, where she was positioning Mandy in the transport tank. "She's a little angled. Is that okay?"

Clay gave Hazel a nudge. "It's your show."

Hazel snapped out of her shock and turned her attention to Mandy. "That's fine, Kat," she said. "Just watch her peck on that far side." Clay watched his not-so-little girl take charge and he smiled.

* * *

When the truck pulled onto the beach, there was a lot to coordinate. Out on the water, Kyle was already positioned in a follow-boat with two other aquarium staff. Once Mandy was released into the ocean, it would be their job to follow her into the deeper waters and make sure she was okay. On the shore, a crowd gathered to watch Mandy's release. Inside the truck, Sawyer tapped Hazel on the shoulder and pointed to three familiar faces. It was the little girl named Mandy with her brother and mother. They were the ones who found the dolphin in the lagoon. Together, they were holding a sign that said "We ♥ Mandy 4-Ever!!!" Sawyer and Hazel smiled and waved.

A few minutes later, Hazel led Kat and Rebecca as they moved Mandy out of the truck. Clay helped the team carry the stretcher down to the shore. "We're getting ready, Kyle," Hazel said into a walkie-talkie.

Kat stroked Mandy on the back as the team waded waist-deep into the water. "Good girl. You're doing great." Mandy responded by giving a strong slap of her tail flukes.

"Whoa, watch out!" Clay called out.

"This is far enough," said Hazel. She looked at

Clay, who gave her a little nod. "Phoebe, how's that transmitter?"

Phoebe checked the transmitter tag on Mandy's dorsal fin. "All good," she reported.

"We're good here, Kyle," said Hazel into the radio. "You guys got a good signal?"

Out in the boat, Kyle checked the GPS screen. "You bet. Nice and strong."

"All right, everyone," Hazel announced. "It's time. Left side—lower on three. One, two, three!"

The team lowered the left side of the stretcher while Clay maneuvered the dolphin into the water. She slid off the stretcher and splashed into the ocean.

"That's it!" Phoebe exclaimed. "Go on, Mandy!"

Mandy rolled onto her back, then onto her front again, getting a feel for the water. Then she gave a big flip of her tail up and down, propelling herself farther into the water. "YES!!" Everyone cheered.

Looking with binoculars, Kyle and his team watched Mandy swim off. Kyle checked his receiver and saw a strong blip on the GPS. "Got her," he said into the radio, observing the dot moving briskly. "And she's really movin'!"

Back on the beach, the little girl Mandy held her sign higher. "Bye, Mandy!" she shouted. "Get home safe!"

Beep! Beep! Beep! went the GPS on the boat. Kyle looked at the screen and frowned. He picked up the radio. "Hang on. Something's coming."

"What do you see?" Hazel replied.

"I . . . don't know yet."

"What do you see, Kyle?" Hazel repeated faster, grabbing a pair of binoculars.

Kyle studied the screen. "It's a school of . . . something. Sharks, maybe. They're coming right at her. And fast—" He looked to the others in his boat, who were watching the screen with a tense focus.

From the shallow water, Hazel, Clay, and Sawyer strained to see if they could spot Mandy or the predators. "They should move in!" Sawyer shouted.

"Wait!" Hazel said, pointing. "There!" She handed Clay the binoculars.

Clay adjusted the binoculars and focused in the

direction Hazel was pointing. "Dolphins," he said, handing the binoculars to Sawyer.

Sawyer was in awe. "It's a whole pod," he said.

"Kyle! They're bottlenose!" Hazel said into the radio.

"You sure?" Kyle asked.

Under the water, Mandy's pod family surrounded the young dolphin. They bumped her with their rostrums and swam circles around her. Mandy was home!

"Look!" Phoebe shouted, pointing at a dolphin leaping out of the water. It was followed by another and another. Suddenly, the team saw Mandy leap out of the water.

"Ho-ly smoke . . ." marveled Kyle.

Clay's face lit up. "Looks like she's getting a hero's welcome."

CHAPTER EIGHT

George scrolled through the X-rays on Clay's laptop one by one, studying each image. The click of the mouse was the only sound filling the houseboat. Finally, the USDA employee pointed to the screen. "This here, on her spine. New inflammation?"

Clay grimaced. "Yeah."

"And curvature's getting worse." George stopped to clean his glasses and think. He had hoped that in the thirty days since his last visit, Clay and his team would have made more progress. "Has anyone else seen these?"

"Just one or two of the staff."

George spotted a coffeemaker. "May I?"

"Sure." Clay walked over and poured him a mug of coffee, and then one for himself.

"You know, I used to run a facility, too. Just like this one."

"I didn't know that," Clay said, handing him a second mug.

"Palm Bay Marine Hospital. Seventeen years. Do you have sugar?"

Clay handed him the sugar bowl.

"Believe me, I know what you're going through," said George, spooning the sugar into his coffee. "Sometimes my job's not much fun." He took a sip. "Congrats on that release, by the way." George lifted his coffee mug, indicating a toast to Clay. "We love to see success. Although, in this case, I guess it's a bit of a double-edged sword." He put down his coffee and started writing on one of the many forms stacked in front of him. Clay put down his coffee and watched in silence. His stomach was too tied in knots.

Sawyer stood on the platform in the dolphin pool brushing the walls and enjoying the quiet. It was the end of the day at the aquarium and most of the visitors had left. Sawyer was relieved to have more mobility in his hand now that the soft cast was off. It felt good to be able to help out more around the aquarium.

"That was nice of you," Hazel said.

Sawyer looked up to where Hazel was standing on the partition separating the two pools. On the other side of her, Winter drifted listlessly in the East Pool. "Huh?" Sawyer mumbled.

"That vet with the prosthetic leg. Letting him see Winter."

"Oh. Right."

Hazel adjusted the long-handled brush in her hands then resumed cleaning the pool walls. "And that volunteer, too." She glanced over to Sawyer. "What was her name?"

"Who?"

"Dark hair . . . pretty . . ." Hazel said, trying to sound indifferent.

"Oh," said Sawyer. "Susie."

Hearing her friends talking, Winter wandered closer to the gates to listen.

Hazel wanted to know more about Sawyer's feelings for Susie—if he had any—but she couldn't figure out how to ask. Instead, she just said, "So, you book your flight yet?"

Sawyer stiffened, but he kept cleaning. "No. I mean, Kyle did, but—I don't know."

Hazel stopped to look at the boy. "What don't you know?"

"I . . . I don't know if I'm going."

"Oh, Sawyer! But you *have* to go!"

"Why? Why does everybody say that?" Sawyer said, his frustration bubbling to the surface.

"It's such a great opportunity—"

"I know it is," he said, cutting her off. "That's all anybody ever says to me anymore. 'Wow, Sawyer! What an opportunity!' I should just wear a T-shirt that says 'I GET IT!'"

Stunned by his outburst, Hazel kept quiet.

"But what am I supposed to do?" Sawyer said softly. "Mandy's gone. Panama's gone. Winter's getting worse." The thought of something happening to Winter because he wasn't there was unbearable. "I can't even go in the water with her anymore. How can I leave now?"

Hazel looked past her cleaning brush and watched Winter swim slowly around the pool. She and Sawyer both seemed so sad. *If only there was something I could do,* she thought. Then she had an idea. "When do you have to tell them?" she asked.

"A week," Sawyer muttered.

But Hazel wasn't really listening. Reaching with her brush handle, she pushed open the gate separating the two pools.

Sawyer looked up. "Hey! What are you doing?"

The two friends watched Winter swim through the gate and into the Main Pool.

"It's gone on long enough," Hazel said quietly.

Sawyer didn't take his eyes off Winter. "We are going to be in so much trouble."

Hazel was determined. "At least we'll know," she said as Winter swam in a big slow circle around the pool. "Hold still."

"I am," Sawyer practically hissed. Of course he was going to hold still. The last thing he wanted to do was upset Winter—again, he thought. He held his breath.

"If she gets aggressive, get out."

"No kidding."

"Just talk to her," advised Hazel.

Sawyer bristled. "Hey, I've known her longer than *you* have."

Hazel took her attention off Winter for a split second to roll her eyes. "Yeah, like, twenty minutes." She glanced over at Sawyer and they started to laugh.

"Okay, shush!" Sawyer whispered, getting serious again. "You know what I mean. Don't be so pushy. I know how to do this."

Hazel stared as Sawyer reached his hand out over the platform. He called out to the dolphin. Winter nudged toward him and looked him in the eye. Hazel was afraid to even blink. *Oh, no, what if I made a huge mistake and Winter attacks Sawyer?* At that moment, Winter raised her head and tweeted.

Hazel gasped. "Tweety Bird!"

Winter bumped Sawyer's bandaged hand with her rostrum and looked up at him. Sawyer realized she wanted to see his wrist, so he dipped it into the water. The dolphin submerged to take a closer look. When she came back to the surface, she tweeted again.

"Answer her!" Hazel encouraged.

Sawyer inhaled and whistled the notes familiar to Winter. She tweeted again.

"Hang on!" Hazel ran over to the basket of toys and pulled out the yellow rubber-duck ring. She scurried over to Sawyer and handed him the toy.

Sawyer slowly held out the ring. Winter inched forward, getting closer and closer to Sawyer. He pushed out the memory of the last time he tried this with the dolphin and she slammed him into the side of the pool. Instead, he concentrated on keeping the ring steady. With one quick motion, Winter came rushing toward him—and speared the ring.

"She did it!" Hazel squealed.

Sawyer let out a long breath as Winter swam around the pool with the ring on her rostrum. When she swung back around to the platform, Sawyer reached out to her again and Winter let him remove the ring. She stayed close to him, so he reached down to pet her. "Hey, girl," he said softly. "Long time no see. Everything okay? We good now?"

Winter replied by snuggling her dorsal fin under his hand. He looked at Hazel. *Is this a good idea?* She nodded.

Sawyer took hold of Winter's fin and she swam forward, pulling him into the water. The boy's face lit up as his old friend towed him across the pool. When the dolphin turned to do a big barrel roll, Sawyer rolled, too. The two were together again.

When Sawyer came up for air, Hazel was grinning widely. *It worked.*

"She's okay!" he called out, swimming over to her. Hazel reached out to give him a high five. But before she knew it, Sawyer had taken her hand and pulled her into the pool.

"Hey!" Hazel said, sputtering.

Sawyer laughed. "Serves you right!"

Hazel took her hand and sent a palmful of water at Sawyer's head. Seeing her friends having a water fight, Winter came over and dipped her head down. She lifted it up quickly and a huge splash of water rained down on Sawyer and Hazel. The kids shrieked with delight. Sawyer took Hazel's hand and laid it on Winter's dorsal fin. As soon as she took hold, Winter pushed off, taking Hazel for a ride around the pool while Sawyer swam next to them. The three of them dove under the water, twirling and gliding together. Sawyer felt happier and more relaxed than he had in weeks. Finally, Winter was acting like herself again.

After a bit, Hazel and Sawyer came to the surface with Winter between them. "That's a good girl. . . ." Sawyer said, stroking the dolphin. From the other side, Hazel began to pet her, too. For a moment, Sawyer's and Hazel's hands touched. They both stopped and looked at each other. Their eyes locked. But before either of them had a chance to speak—

"HAZEL!"

—the kids spun around. It was Clay. And he was furious.

* * *

"It wasn't his fault, Dad," Hazel said, standing with Sawyer by the side of the pool. They were wrapped in towels with their clothes still dripping. "It was my decision."

"I don't care whose decision it was. It was dangerous," Clay scolded. "These are wild animals— not pets. I told you *specifically*."

"But you weren't here," Sawyer blurted. "And I know Winter better than anyone. So we made our *own* decision. And she was fine. Don't blame Hazel for anything." Sawyer took a breath. "If you need to blame somebody, blame me."

Clay sighed. Sawyer and Hazel weren't kids anymore. They could make grown-up decisions and they would have to handle bad news, too. "Guys . . ." he said. "It doesn't matter. . . ." He looked at Hazel, who was glancing at the wall clock. She gave her father a panicked look.

Clay checked out the time and frowned. "I know this is a bad time," he said, "but I have to tell you that George Hatton came by." Sawyer tensed. "He wrote a new violation . . . and a transfer order." Clay held up a piece of paper. "They're moving Winter to a marine park in Texas."

CHAPTER NINE

Out in the parking lot a few minutes later, Sawyer walked his bike. He didn't have the energy to ride it. The last half hour had been a roller coaster. Being able to swim with Winter again made him happier than he had been in weeks. But the thought of her leaving CMA was devastating. *What are we going to do? How can we get George Hatton to let Winter stay?* His thoughts were interrupted when a familiar car pulled into the lot and drove up next to him.

"Mom?"

"Hi, sweetheart," Lorraine said, reaching her hand out the window and putting it on Sawyer's arm.

"I'm sorry I'm late, I was just—"

"No, no, it's fine. I just had this sudden craving for that Jamaican grouper they have over at the Island Way Grill. What do you say? Grab some dinner?"

Sawyer was quiet on the ride to the restaurant. He didn't feel much like talking. He was still lost in thought when Lorraine parked the car and they walked into the restaurant.

"Oh, good," Lorraine said, "they're not crowded."

Sawyer tried to take a look around. "How can you tell? It's so dark—"

Snap! Suddenly, the lights went on, momentarily blinding Sawyer.

"SURPRISE!"

Sawyer's aunt Alyce, his cousin Kyle, and tons of his friends from CMA were there with their arms in the air, standing under a colorful banner that read "Congratulations on Your New Adventures!" Sawyer blinked in the bright lights then looked at his mother, who was smiling at him. He knew how excited she was to do something for him. But the last thing Sawyer felt like doing was celebrating. He did his best to smile back.

After his guests had come over to congratulate him at the door, Sawyer made his way over to the drinks table, where Hazel, Kyle, Kat, and Phoebe were gathered.

"You must be so thrilled," Phoebe said.

"Um . . . yeah," said Sawyer.

"When do you guys leave?" Kat asked.

Sawyer and Hazel exchanged a look.

"Twenty-third," Kyle answered. He grinned at his cousin. "We're on the noon flight from Tampa."

Over by the buffet table, Lorraine and her sister Alyce were getting some food. "You must be so happy for him, Lorraine," Alyce said, putting a spoonful of rice on her plate.

"I am. I really am," said Lorraine, picking up a pair of tongs to grab a piece of grouper.

"And such a nice turnout. Shows you how much people love that boy."

Lorraine nodded and put her hand to her mouth. Suddenly, she burst into tears.

"Oh, Lorraine!" her sister said.

"I'm fine, I'm fine," Lorraine said, and quickly wiped her eyes. She reached into her purse to get a tissue but lost control of her plate, spilling the grouper onto the table. "Oh, shoot—"

Alyce put down her plate. "I'll get it."

But Lorraine just got more flustered. "It's okay, I've got it," she said, putting down her own plate, then putting her bag on top of the rice.

Alyce took her sister by the shoulders and gave her a hug. "It's okay," she said.

"I'm sorry," Lorraine gushed. "It's just—he just got so big so fast!"

Alyce handed her sister a napkin to wipe her eyes. "I know. Same with Kyle. One day he's your little boy, then all of a sudden—he's a big, ugly man."

Lorraine smiled at her sister while dabbing her eyes. She always knew how to lift her spirits. "Kyle's very handsome."

"Oh, you know what I mean."

"I *want* Sawyer to go, I do. I just . . ." Lorraine said, starting to well up again. "I don't want him to *go*."

* * *

Later that evening, Sawyer sat down on a bench with a paper plate of cake. He picked up his fork and took a bite, but he didn't have much of an appetite. He put the fork back down.

"Hey."

Sawyer looked up and was startled to see Dr. McCarthy.

"I never pass up a free meal," the doctor said, taking a seat beside Sawyer. He reached into his coat pocket and pulled out a little wooden box. "I got you something," he said, handing it over. Sawyer took the box, feeling puzzled.

Dr. McCarthy shrugged. "Going-away present. Old Chinese custom. Open it."

Sawyer lifted the box lid and pulled out an antique silver pocket watch. No one had ever given him something like this before. "It's beautiful," he said. He ran his thumb over the watch face, then took his forefinger and thumb and began to wind the knob. Nothing happened.

Dr. McCarthy pointed to the watch with his thumb. "The thing crapped out years ago. Belonged to my uncle Bill. It's been sitting in my garage since the Nixon administration."

"Oh. Well. Thanks." Sawyer thought it was a little odd to give a broken gift, but then again, Dr. McCarthy was a little odd, too.

"Hit it," the doctor said. "Hit the thing."

Sawyer looked back at the watch. He gave it a gentle smack and it started to tick. "Hey, there it goes." But a few seconds later, it stopped. Sawyer smacked it again. The watch ticked a couple of times, then stopped.

"You see the problem?" Dr. McCarthy asked.

Sawyer had a feeling he knew what was coming. He squinted at the doctor. "I'm about to get a lesson here, aren't I?"

The two grinned.

"The watch is beautiful, but my guess is that it sat in that box so long that it finally just stopped," said Dr. McCarthy.

"Okay . . ."

Dr. McCarthy took the watch from Sawyer. "Shaking the watch up a little, that's the only thing that gets it moving forward." He shook it and it started to tick once more. "The world is too big—and there's too many possibilities—to spend your life sitting in a box." He looked around at Sawyer's friends and family, everyone who had come out to celebrate with him. "No matter how nice that box might be."

Sawyer looked around the room and he nodded. "Thanks, Dr. McCarthy."

The doctor smiled. "My pleasure."

On the other side of the party, Hazel walked over to get some cake. Talking with people from CMA and having to keep the transfer order a secret was exhausting. Hazel was trying to take a quiet moment to herself when Susie approached.

"Uh, Hazel?" Susie said. "Hi, I'm Susie—I'm a new volunteer."

Hazel was startled but then she nodded. She knew who Susie was and knew Sawyer did, too.

"Um, I don't know if they'll have Internet on the boat where Sawyer's going," Susie said nervously. "But I was just wondering—do you mind if I friend him on Facebook?"

"No," Hazel answered. She thought for a second. "Why would I mind?"

"Oh!" Susie's eyes grew large. "I thought you two might be—"

Hazel realized what Susie meant and tried to laugh. "Oh. No, gosh. Whatever gave you *that* idea—?"

But Susie rushed on, "And can I friend you, too? I admire you guys both *so* much!"

"Oh, okay." Hazel felt herself starting to smile. She felt lighter all of a sudden, although she didn't quite understand why. "Sure," she told Susie. "Absolutely."

* * *

While Hazel was feeling better momentarily, her father, Clay, was feeling worse. He kept reading the transfer order again and again. Finally, he checked his watch. He wasn't sure Sawyer would even want to see him at his party, but he had to show his support. Clay threw the transfer order to the side of his desk and stood up to go. On his way out, he stopped at Winter's pool and watched her float out from under the platform. Memories of Winter's rescue, the struggles with her prosthetic tail, and her joyful performance on Save Winter Day flashed through his mind. *Did I make a huge mistake letting Mandy back into the wild? Why didn't I keep Mandy just a* little *longer?*

The buzz of his cell phone stopped Clay's flood of regrets. "Hello, this is Clay Haskett." The other side of the line crackled. "Hello? Who's this? You're breaking up." Clay moved away from the pool and toward his office to try to get a better signal. "Yes, hello?" His forehead wrinkled as he listened to the caller shout information in his ear. Then, with a bright smile that practically lit up the aquarium, he shouted in reply, "Do we? You bet your life we do!"

* * *

"Guys, there's an emergency." Phoebe ran over to where Kat, Rebecca, Sawyer, and Hazel were gathered at the party. She had just gotten off the phone with Clay.

"What's going on?" asked Sawyer, putting down his plate.

"Clay needs us. Now."

Sawyer and Hazel exchanged a worried look. *No, please don't let anything be wrong with Winter.*

"Marine Fisheries—they picked up a stranding," Phoebe added. "They're on their way."

The team immediately kicked into gear. Sawyer ran over to tell his mother that a beached dolphin had been found and was being taken to CMA. He and the other staff had to get back to the aquarium right away. Within fifteen minutes, Phoebe, Kat, and Rebecca were already in their wet suits back at CMA. At the medical pools, Reed and Clay drained the water to prepare for the wounded animal's arrival. "I need this down to four feet," Clay explained.

"We got it," said Reed.

"Clay! I got him!" Phoebe said, holding up her cell phone. She put it back to her ear. "Steve? Can you hear me?" She squinted, straining to hear the other end of the line. "What's your ETA? . . . Okay . . . Twenty minutes?"

Clay nodded. They would be ready.

"Say again, Steve," Phoebe continued. "You're

breaking up." She listened for a moment, then her eyes jumped to Clay. "It's a juvenile . . . Male?" Just then, Hazel and Sawyer approached. Phoebe lowered the phone. "Clay?" She looked utterly amazed. "It's a female."

CHAPTER TEN

Down in the CMA parking lot less than twenty minutes later, Hazel filmed the huge group that had gathered. The CMA staff and volunteers, as well as Sawyer's party guests who had come over with hopes of getting a glimpse of the rescued dolphin, stood together.

"All right, everybody," Clay commanded. "The minute they arrive, there will be one voice only—and that will be mine." He scanned the group. "I need a stretcher team. Phoebe, I want you with me at the head. And I'll need some strong backs."

Kyle stepped forward. "Here's one right here," he said, raising his hand.

Clay nodded and gestured for Kyle to join him at his side. He looked back to the crowd for one other important person. "Sawyer."

Hazel turned the camera just in time to catch Sawyer's stunned expression. He would never have guessed that Clay would choose him. He assumed Clay would think he was too young, and besides, wasn't Clay still angry with him?

Clay gave the boy a soft smile and looked him squarely in the eye. "I want you beside me."

Lorraine stood filled with pride next to Dr. McCarthy and watched her son join Kyle on Clay's stretcher team. Kyle seemed stronger than ever despite needing a brace for his leg, and Sawyer continued to inspire her every day. She was so proud of these two young men. She peeked up at Dr. McCarthy. *He must be thinking the same thing*, she thought. "Hope this one's not missing any pieces," said the doctor. "If it's lost its head, there's not much I can do." Lorraine laughed. *Could Dr. McCarthy ever be thinking the same thing as me? Nope.*

In the next moment, Lorraine heard someone announce, "They're here!" A blue truck with Harbor Marine Rescue on the side rumbled into the parking lot with its emergency lights flashing. It screeched to a stop in front of Clay. Clay went around to the back of the truck and opened the doors to see a small dolphin lying on its side on a yellow stretcher. The rescue workers in the truck sprang into action.

"How's she doing, Steve?" Clay asked.

Steve wrapped up the dolphin in several blankets and lifted her off the stretcher. "She's stiffening up. Might not make it. Gotta get her in the water fast. . . ." he said, lifting her out of the truck.

Still filming, Hazel gasped from behind the camera. "Dad, she's little!"

But Clay was only focused on getting the dolphin into the medical pool as quickly as possible. "I'll just take her," he said to Kyle as he took the dolphin from Steve and carried her in his arms. "Get the stretcher ready up top!"

Hazel, the stretcher team, and the Harbor Rescue workers followed Clay and the dolphin into the building and straight up to the medical pools. After a few minutes, the dolphin was back in a stretcher.

"Get the hooks on," Clay instructed. Kyle and Sawyer quickly attached the hooks to the stretcher while Phoebe and Kat rushed into the water. Kyle double-checked that each hook was securely fastened, then signaled to Reed that they were ready. Reed shot a look toward Clay to confirm everything was set. Clay nodded. "Here we go, everyone." Reed hit the button to hoist the stretcher into the air.

"That's enough," Clay said. He and Kyle let the stretcher swing gently over the water.

"Okay, down now," Clay guided Reed. "Easy . . . easy does it."

From the pool, Phoebe and Kat reached up and grabbed the stretcher to steady it. Together they helped lower it into the water. Just as the stretcher hit the water, the dolphin let out a loud whistle.

Hazel peeked her head out from behind the camera again. "Listen! She's vocalizing!" Hazel quickly got back in position and adjusted the camera lens, zooming in on Phoebe and Kat as they slid the dolphin out of the stretcher and into their arms.

"Good work, everybody," said Clay. He turned to the Harbor Rescue crew. "Well done, guys." He returned his attention to the pool, where everyone else was looking at Kat and Phoebe cradling the dolphin in their arms. "Now all we can do is hope. . . ."

Hazel lowered her camera. "That's her name!"

"What is?" asked Clay, lowering his eyebrows.

"Hope!" Hazel looked pleased. "I just named her." Then she glanced over to Sawyer.

"Sure," her friend agreed.

Clay addressed the group. "Everybody, say hello to Hope."

Up in the rooftop dolphin pools, Winter could also hear the whistles of the young dolphin. Winter bobbed to the surface of the water, and when she heard Hope vocalizing, she tweeted back.

CHAPTER ELEVEN

The next few weeks were a blur of activity at the aquarium. To everyone's relief, Hope was recovering at a rapid pace. She was given a full workup of tests within her first few days. The staff determined that she was too young to have learned from her mom how to survive in the wild and therefore could never be released. As soon as Clay had verified Hope's test results and medical records, he called George Hatton requesting that the transfer order for Winter be postponed. But George had to see Winter and Hope together himself. He would be coming in a few days and the staff had a lot to do to prepare.

When word got out that a new dolphin had been rescued whose presence might make it possible for Winter to stay in Clearwater, news teams started reporting every day on progress at the aquarium. But it turned out that Hope wasn't the only animal getting buzz. While Hope would not be able to return to the wild, Mavis the sea turtle was fully recovered and ready to head back home. One morning, when the sun had just crept up over the horizon, a crowd was already gathered at the beach surrounding Rebecca, Hazel, and Sawyer. The trio carried Mavis wrapped up in a folded rubber mat, and shuffled down the shore while a television news cameraman trailed them.

"Whoa!" the cameraman called out suddenly. A pelican had just jumped into his shot then scurried after Sawyer, Hazel, Rebecca, and Mavis.

Sawyer turned back to see what was causing the commotion. "Rufus! Cut it out!" he scolded. A few feet away from where the waves were hitting the sand,

Sawyer and the girls set down the mat. Seeing his opportunity, Rufus scuttled forward and nipped at the mat.

Hazel shooed him away. "Get back! Go, go!" She held out her arms like a basketball player on defense, blocking the pelican so Rebecca and Sawyer could unwrap the turtle. As soon as she was free, Mavis's instinct kicked in and she started shuffling toward the water.

"There you go, Mavis," Rebecca said with encouragement.

Aaawp! Rufus screeched.

Hazel spun her head around to cheer on the turtle while still fending off Rufus. "Go, Mavis! Go!"

As Mavis reached the water and scrambled into the shallow surf, the crowd started rooting louder. "You can do it, Mavis!" "Go, Mavis!" "Yay, Mavis!"

Rufus paced back and forth, flapping his wings. Finally, he couldn't take it anymore. He bolted around Hazel and lifted off into the air.

"Hey!" Hazel cried, waving her arms.

The bird flew low right over Sawyer and Rebecca. If they had raised their hands in time they could have touched him. "Rufus, no!" Rebecca shouted.

But Rufus zoomed on ahead. He spied Mavis's shell, just barely visible in between the breaking waves. *Squawk! Squawk! Squawk!*

Down below, Mavis swam farther out to sea, her body disappearing under the waves then reappearing again. Rufus circled overhead. When he was directly above her, he swooped back toward shore.

"That crazy bird," Hazel murmured. *I guess he just wanted to see Mavis off himself. After all, he* was *the one who technically found her.* Hazel smiled thinking back on all the times Rufus got himself in trouble. He could be annoying, but deep down, she liked having him around. She looked up as he approached the shore. The pelican locked eyes with her. *Squawk!* Hazel expected him to dive back down to the sand and waddle over to her. But to her surprise, the pelican banked to his right and made a huge turn heading back to the sea. "Rufus—no!" *He isn't coming back.*

He is going with Mavis! Hazel's eyes shifted back and forth from the sky to the sea, watching the two animal friends disappear in the distance.

* * *

That night, Sawyer sat in his bed trying to read, but none of the words were sinking in. All he could think about was George Hatton's visit in two days. Tomorrow the team was going to put Winter and Hope together for the first time. Putting a wild animal with another animal always had potential dangers. But with Winter missing her tail, nobody knew how Hope would react. She could try to hurt Winter or end up hurting herself. Winter might be upset that Hope wasn't Panama and act out. Adding to the pressure, if the two dolphins couldn't get along, Winter would be transferred to Texas. They only had a few days to make sure Winter stayed. Sawyer pushed the thought out of his head—again.

"Hey, son," his mother called from his bedroom door. "Ready for tomorrow?"

Sawyer sighed. *So much for not thinking about it,* he thought. He shrugged.

Lorraine studied her son. *Maybe I should just leave him alone, but I have to think of his future.* "You know . . ." she said, stepping into the room. "It's almost the end of the month—"

Sawyer wouldn't let her finish. "Mom, I know. Dr. Aslan needs an answer."

"Well, he does. And the longer we—"

"But I don't know!" Sawyer blurted out. "How can I tell him if I don't know what's going to happen with Winter?"

"Honey . . ." Lorraine said, sitting on Sawyer's bed. "They're not going to hold your spot forever. Sometimes in life, you just have to make a decision."

Sawyer's face was hard. *If only it were so easy.* "Don't, Mom, okay? I get it."

Lorraine swallowed. "Well. We'll see how tomorrow goes." She stood up and headed toward the door. Before she walked out, she turned back to look at Sawyer one more time. It was tough seeing him so troubled. "I love you, Sawyer," she said with a gentle tone. "More than anything. You know that."

Sawyer let out a long exhale. He knew his mom was just trying to help. "I know, Mom. I love you, too."

When he was alone again, Sawyer looked around his room. *Maybe I should just go to sleep,* he thought. He had to be at the aquarium at dawn to get ready. Sawyer grabbed his alarm clock off his shelf, checked the time, and put it back.

Tick, tick, tick, tick.

Huh? Sawyer looked back at the shelf and noticed the box from Dr. McCarthy. He took it down and lifted the lid. *Tick, tick, tick, tick.* The watch was running.

CHAPTER TWELVE

Sawyer woke up in darkness and was at CMA as the sun's first rays touched the sky. He stood in the Great Hall of the aquarium along with every CMA staff member and volunteer. Winter was special to all of them; they all desperately wanted to see her get along with Hope. They all desperately wanted to see her stay in Clearwater.

"Okay, everyone," Phoebe said into a microphone, calling everyone to attention. "Now, remember, today has to feel like a normal day. . . . The dolphins will have their regular sessions. Kat will have Hope, and

Sawyer will have Winter. You all know your assignments." She surveyed the room. "Gate-minders?" She nodded as two staff members raised their hands. "Good. Where's Kyle?" Kyle waved. "Kyle's our safety. If anyone is in trouble, his word is law." The group murmured their understanding. Phoebe handed Sawyer the microphone.

Sawyer cleared his throat. "First of all, I want to thank everybody for your hard work and preparation for this moment." He paused while the crowd applauded. "But remember, no matter how much we love Winter and Hope, they are wild animals. They can bite, or rake each other with their teeth, and even draw blood. They can head-butt or take a cheap shot when the other one's not looking. That's how they establish dominance in the wild. It's natural, but it can be rough." His eyes scanned the faces of rapt listeners. "Reed, Rebecca—you have the nets, right?" Reed gave him a thumbs-up and Rebecca nodded. "If they attack, you divers get in and get that net between them—fast. But if it goes right and they accept each other, you'll see parallel swimming." He held out his hands a few inches apart and moved them in an S-like motion. "It'll be easy, natural, relaxed behavior. If anything looks aggressive, remember our goal is safety first—theirs *and ours*."

Sawyer took a moment to make sure everyone understood the seriousness of the experiment. "Any final questions?"

Clay raised his hand. "I have one."

Huh? What could I know that Dr. Clay doesn't? "Dr. Clay?" asked Sawyer with a puzzled expression.

Dr. Clay just grinned and asked, "When did you get so bossy?"

Sawyer looked sheepish. *I've learned so much over the last few years*, he thought. *Maybe I am ready for some new adventures after all.*

* * *

After his speech, Sawyer and the rest of the staff went to get in position. Kyle joined the medics. Clay and Phoebe checked on Winter in the East Pool and Hope in the Main Pool. Reed and Rebecca inspected the nets one last time. Sawyer was hurrying toward the pool carrying a cooler of fish for Winter when he tripped and smashed right into Hazel loading film in her camera.

"Oh! Sorry—" Sawyer stammered.

"No, my fault. I must have . . . I just, uh . . ." Hazel said, stuttering. She had just realized that, in the commotion, her hand had landed on Sawyer's chest. She blushed and pulled her hand back. "Sorry—um . . . good luck today," she said and rushed off.

A few minutes later, a hush had fallen over the pool area. Everyone was at their station ready for Kat and Sawyer to begin. At the edge of the pool, Hazel grabbed a long pole attached to a special underwater camera, lowered it into the water, and started filming.

Without any sudden movement or loud sounds, Kat and Sawyer approached the pools. In the Main Pool, Kat gave Hope a signal to stand upright in the water. When Hope followed the instructive cue and opened her mouth, Kat squirted some water in playfully. Then she hopped in to join her. Over in the East Pool, Sawyer slid into the water and started to pet Winter gently. "Hey, girl . . ." The dolphin nudged toward the boy's hand and tweeted.

"Everybody set?" Phoebe said in an authoritative but calm tone. Clay double-checked everyone's position. They looked good.

"All good, Phoebe," he said.

"Okay." She looked to the gate-minders. "Open it."

Sawyer held his breath as the gate-minders pushed the barrier out of the way. He guided the dolphin toward the gate. Winter dipped down and glided forward. When she went through the gate into the Main Pool, she hesitated. Kat had released Hope.

It didn't take long for the dolphins to find each other underwater. Within moments, they were face-to-face, bumping rostrums. Winter made a biting motion and Phoebe started to move in when Clay stopped her. "Just wait."

The two animals continued checking each other out. Winter stayed still while Hope circled her. When Hope reached Winter's peduncle—the big muscle between a dolphin's dorsal fin and tail—Hope echolocated. But the echoes that bounced back to her didn't make any sense. *Where is this other dolphin's tail?* Hope didn't understand and started to panic. She whirled around so fast that her tail flukes smacked right into Winter's peduncle.

Hope didn't know what to do, so she just swam as fast as she possibly could around the perimeter of the pool. Winter followed her awkwardly, swishing her tail from side to side. She was so eager to get to know this young new dolphin. When Hope swung back around, passing her, Winter tried to bump her with her rostrum.

"No, Winter!" Sawyer shouted.

But Hope had already frantically spun around and snapped at Winter. The older dolphin tried to give Hope another friendly nudge but it only angered her. Hope smacked her tail again and again, then leaped and landed back in the water with a smash.

"Get 'em apart," Clay directed.

The net team started forward, but Winter was already on the move.

"Wait, wait!" Sawyer yelped, holding his arms out. Winter was bolting for the gate and he didn't want to traumatize her further by having the net team capture her. She zoomed through the gate back into the East Pool and shot under the platform, where no one could see her.

* * *

Clay and his team were emotionally exhausted. They had been preparing for Hope and Winter's meeting for weeks and the outcome was a crushing disappointment. All afternoon, Sawyer tried to get Winter to come out from under the platform, but she refused. She wouldn't even come out to eat. At the end of the day, the staff ordered some takeout for dinner and piled around Clay's computer in the Great Hall to figure out what to do next.

"Okay, so this is the underwater footage from this morning. . . ." Hazel explained, pressing a key on Clay's keyboard.

Phoebe studied the screen. "So, at first, Winter was fine. She held in the gate—"

"—being territorial," Clay added.

"'It's my gate, not yours,'" Reed suggested.

"Then Hope circles Winter. . . ." Phoebe continued.

"There. Freeze it. Look!" said Sawyer.

Hazel tapped a key to rewind the video, then froze it.

On-screen, Hope faced Winter's peduncle. Phoebe leaned forward in her chair. "She's echolocating."

Hazel pressed PLAY once again and the team watched as Hope reacted with agitation. "She realizes Winter has no tail," said Hazel.

"And she doesn't like that," Sawyer stated. "Watch. . . ." On the video, Winter was now swimming with her tail's side-to-side stroke, and Hope was getting more and more upset. "When Winter starts swimming—"

"It freaked Hope out," Kyle said, finishing Sawyer's thought.

Hazel hit PAUSE.

"Well, it is unnatural, that motion. . . ." Clay said, thinking aloud.

Phoebe leaned onto the table and put her hand to her chin. "But there's nothing we can do about that, that's just how she swims. . . ."

Clay's eyes met Sawyer's.

"Not always . . ." Sawyer said. Suddenly, everyone had the same idea. "Exactly . . . What if . . . what if Winter wore the tail?"

Everyone started talking at once, each voicing a strong opinion.

"Oh, no," Phoebe said. "That'd freak out Hope even more. . . ."

"It might not. . . ." Kyle countered.

"She's never seen anything like it in the wild. She'd go nuts," Kat argued.

"A huge contraption on her tail . . ." said Rebecca.

"If she smacks Hope with it . . ." Phoebe said.

"She is awful little. . . ." Reed said quietly.

"And Winter *has* been aggressive lately. . . ." Kat reminded everyone.

Clay held up his hand. "Hold it, everyone. Hold it." The crew got quiet. "Everything you're saying is true. The tail would give Winter a more natural swimming motion. But if Winter clocks Hope with it, it's game over." To everyone's surprise, he turned to Sawyer. "What do you think? She's been aggressive before. Think she'll do it again?"

Sawyer felt the eyes of the CMA senior staff boring into him. He tried to ignore them and took a moment to think. "No . . . that was my fault. I pushed her too fast. She wasn't ready." He looked around and saw doubt on several faces.

"Look, I know Winter," Sawyer said. "And she's fine now, I can see it. I see it in her eyes and the way she moves. And the way she is with me. She's like she always was. She never meant any harm and she never will." He took a deep breath. "If we don't give her this chance, what *do* we do? Give up? I don't want to spend the rest of my life knowing we didn't even try."

The staff was quiet. To Sawyer, the next minute felt like an eternity. Finally, Hazel voiced her opinion on the matter for the first time. "Sawyer's right." She looked at Clay, seeming more grown-up than ever. Clay nodded. He knew Hazel was taking all the important information into account.

"Tomorrow, eight a.m. With the tail," Clay declared. "If anyone objects, speak up now."

No one said a word.

CHAPTER THIRTEEN

Tension was high the next morning. As Lorraine pulled into the CMA parking lot with Kyle and Sawyer, their car was surrounded by swarms of news crews. Reporters hurried over, firing questions through the windows of the car. Sawyer's eyes expanded, taking in the crowds of people wearing T-shirts and buttons with a logo of a dolphin's tail and reading "Hope for Winter."

"Guess word got out," said Kyle.

Lorraine pulled into a parking spot slowly, taking care not to hit anyone. When the three got out of the car, the reporters attacked.

"Sawyer, we heard you're trying to pair Winter and Hope!"

"We heard it failed yesterday!"

"Is it true they attacked each other?"

"There's an aquarium in Texas advertising Winter's on her way there!"

"Is it true? Are we going to lose Winter forever?"

Sawyer felt his throat closing in.

"You guys get inside," Kyle said, stepping in between the reporters and his cousin. "I got this."

By eight a.m., the same team as the day before gathered by the dolphin pools—with one exception. Dr. McCarthy lifted his metal case and set it down on top of a nearby table. He opened the case and revealed a new prosthetic tail with black plastic flukes. "Just finished at four this morning. It's a more streamlined design with carbon-fiber joints, and I made the flukes darker, so we can track the movement better. Plus—as you'll notice," the doctor said with a twinkle in his eye, "it's more floppy." He took a step back, clearly pleased with himself, while the others leaned in to take a closer look.

Sawyer picked up the tail and ran his thumb against the flukes. "More like the real thing," he said admiringly.

"How'd you get the edges so soft?" Clay asked.

Dr. McCarthy smirked. "Three jars of meat tenderizer and a Louisville Slugger. And that's not all. . . ." He opened a smaller case and took out a new gel sleeve.

Hazel was amazed. Years ago, it had taken several tries before Winter would wear the prosthetic tail Dr. McCarthy had made. Winter had to wear a special gel-filled sleeve on her stump so that they could attach the prosthetic tail to her body without hurting her. Sawyer had been the one to realize it was the gel sleeve that Winter found most uncomfortable. Once Dr. McCarthy determined the right gel formula,

Winter accepted wearing the plastic tail and started swimming with an up-and-down motion again, ceasing the damage to her spine.

"Is that a new gel formula, too?" asked Hazel.

Dr. McCarthy pretended to look offended. "Naw, kid! Same formula. I just made a fresh batch. Don't get greedy." Hazel laughed along with the rest of the team.

Just then, Hope whistled from the Main Pool and Winter tweeted in response. Dr. McCarthy nodded his head in their direction. "They're just a couple of chicks talking trash over the fence!"

Within a few minutes, the crew members were in position, checking the nets, the gate, the camera equipment, and the animals. Sawyer and Phoebe took the new tail and sleeve over to Winter in the East Pool. She hopped up onto the platform and looked at the tail calmly. But as soon as Phoebe started to slide on the sleeve, Winter began to thrash.

"Easy, Winter. Easy, girl," Sawyer said in a soothing tone.

Winter settled down but remained skittish.

"You've gotta wear it now. It's the most important time ever," he whispered. "And see? It's new. Dr. McCarthy made it special, just for today." Winter looked over at the doctor. "See? There he is. He stayed up all night making this for you."

Dr. McCarthy peered over the platform. Winter padded over to him. She put her face right in front of the doctor's and let out a long, loud raspberry sound. Dr. McCarthy jumped back, wiping off his face. "My sentiments exactly," he muttered. Sawyer put his hand over his mouth to hide his smile.

* * *

By the time the team was just about ready to go, the rooftop deck was packed. Susie and the other CMA volunteers were crammed together, many wearing "H+W" shirts and buttons. While Sawyer was pleased to see Bethany Hamilton had come out to support Winter, he was nervous to see George Hatton, Phil Hordern, and the rest of the board of directors.

Outside in the parking lot, groups of fans had joined the news crews waiting for updates and information from the roof.

"All right," said Phoebe from the East Pool platform. She stroked Winter's back, glanced at Sawyer, then called over to Clay. "Tail's on."

"'Atta girl," Sawyer said.

"Okay, good. Kat?" Clay said, looking over to the Main Pool. She gave him a thumbs-up.

Clay turned to his father, standing with the divers.

"Ready when you are," said Reed.

Clay cleared his throat. "Okay, let's get her off the platform."

Sawyer and Phoebe slipped into the pool and gave Winter the signal to join them. Once she was in the water, Winter took a minute to get accustomed to the new tail. She took a lap around the pool. *Swish up. Swish down. Swish up. Swish down.* Feeling good, she swam back to her friends and tweeted.

"Hear that?" Kat whispered to Hope in the Main Pool. "That's Winter."

"All right, everyone," Clay said. "If anybody's not ready, speak now."

Sawyer braced himself, but the only sound he heard was water lapping the sides of the pools. He looked at Clay and swallowed. "Let's do it." At Clay's nod of approval, Sawyer guided Winter gently toward the gate-minders, who were sliding open the gate. He let Winter go and watched her dive down and over to the Main Pool.

The dolphin coasted to the middle and stopped underwater. Kat watched as Hope swam off to investigate. She met Winter in the center and the two dolphins stared at each other, rostrum-to-rostrum.

"It's a face-off," said Kyle to Dr. McCarthy in a hushed tone.

"Showdown at high noon," the doctor murmured back.

Clay glanced across the pool at Phil Hordern and George Hatton. They both shared the same tense expression.

After a few seconds, Hope started to circle Winter. Once again, she stopped when she reached Winter's back. Winter waved the tail slowly up and down, making the prosthetic glint in the water. Just as she had the day before, Hope sent out a call and studied the echoes that came back to her. Up on the deck, Hazel held her breath and tried to keep the camera steady. Everyone—from Dr. McCarthy, Kyle, and Lorraine to Phil, George, and Bethany Hamilton—kept their eyes glued on the two dolphins.

Suddenly, Hope spun away from Winter's tail and took off to the side of the pool.

The crowd took a quick inhale and looked at Clay. *This is bad.* "Clay . . ." Phoebe said, anxious to get the team ready for an emergency intervention. Reed and the net team stepped forward.

"Hang on." Clay focused on Hope. In her agitation, the young dolphin had begun to swim swift laps around the pool. To everyone's surprise, Winter launched into high gear and chased after Hope. When Winter caught up to her, Hope whipped around and stopped. *What is going on?* Hope thought. *This other dolphin's tail is definitely different, but she moves the same. Is it safe to be around her?* Hope stared at this strange creature and examined her closely. *Should I try to talk to her?* Hope lifted her head and whistled. Winter voiced her Tweety Bird sound in reply. For a moment, the two dolphins were suspended in the water.

But in the next, Winter turned away and dove to the bottom of the pool. Hope wheeled around to the opposite direction, abandoning the surface of the water. Both dolphins were deep in the pool and out of sight.

"What's happening?" Lorraine said, craning her neck forward to see farther into the pool. "I can't see them."

"Clay?" asked Phoebe, the panic in her voice rising.

"Nobody move," he instructed, scanning the water for the slightest movement.

Everyone struggled to see what would happen next. The viewers who were sitting down stood up.

The ones who were already standing went on tiptoes.

Suddenly, Sawyer jumped and pointed to the pool. "Here they come!"

Winter's back broke through the surface first. Then Hope appeared right next to her. The dolphins lapped the pool, swimming shoulder to shoulder in perfect sync, as if they had been swimming together for years.

"She's . . . she's accepting," Sawyer said incredulously.

The crowd burst into exhilarated applause. *It worked!*

"Woooooohooooooo!" shouted Kyle.

"Well, I'll be darned," said George, shaking his head.

Even Dr. McCarthy couldn't restrain himself. "Man, I love those fish!" he exclaimed.

"Oh, come on," Lorraine said with a laugh. "You know very well they're not fish!"

"Hey," Dr. McCarthy said, straightening his shoulders and resuming his usual curmudgeonly tone. "If it *looks* like a fish, and *smells* like a fish . . ."

Down in the parking lot, no one was holding back their excitement. Mandy jumped up and down with her brother, squeaking, "They like each other! They like each other!"

On the other side of the roof, members of the CMA board were congratulating Phil Hordern and patting him on the back. From a corner in the back, George caught Clay's eye and raised his arm as if holding a glass. *A toast to you!* he seemed to say. Clay smiled and raised his arm, "toasting" back.

Hazel kept her camera focused on the animals. Without warning, Hope turned and leaped over Winter, who reacted by spinning around and zipping after her. "They're playing!" Hazel squealed.

But Winter surprised everyone by swimming past Hope and going after Sawyer. *SPLASH!*

"Whoa!" Sawyer sputtered, blinking the water out of his eyes. Winter playfully head-butted him in the chest, then splashed him again. Hope swam over, wanting to join in the fun. She leapt in front of

Sawyer and landed with an even bigger splash.

"Eek!" shouted Hazel from the platform. She was soaked! Kyle got an idea. He quickly took the camera from Hazel—and pushed her into the water! Hope was thrilled. There were so many friends to play with! Without setting down the camera, Kyle reached down to grab a rubber ball from a basket of toys and threw it into the pool. Hazel caught it and went to toss it to Sawyer, but Winter was too quick. She jumped in between them and bounced the ball off her rostrum toward Hope. The four gleeful friends lit up the pool, splashing and playing as the audience on the deck laughed and cheered them on.

CHAPTER FOURTEEN

Sawyer sat back and let his head fall against the headrest in the backseat of his mom's car. He felt like he was sitting down for the first time in two weeks. Ever since the successful meeting between Winter and Hope, Sawyer had been spending every possible second with Hazel and the dolphins. Only now that he was on the way to the Tampa airport with his mom and Kyle could he feel butterflies in his stomach.

Sawyer glanced out the window and realized they were passing CMA. At the same time, his cell phone buzzed. Sawyer looked down at the screen and read a text from Hazel: "Look to your left."

"Hey, Mom, can we stop for a second?" he asked.

Lorraine looked over to Kyle in the passenger seat, but he just raised his eyebrows and shrugged. He didn't know what was going on either. Lorraine pulled the car over on the side of the highway and turned to her son. *Is he having second thoughts about going to SEA Semester?* Sawyer, however, wasn't looking at her. He was staring at CMA off in the distance. Hazel was standing on the CMA roof, stretching her arms up high and waving at the car.

Sawyer, Lorraine, and Kyle squinted in the morning sunlight and watched Hazel duck down out of sight. All of a sudden, a big spot of green burst over the roof, followed by a spot of blue, then orange, then green. Sawyer blinked, and in an instant the sky above CMA was filled with brightly colored helium balloons that formed a huge archway. Suspended from the center was a banner that said "We ♥ Sawyer 4-Ever!!!"

Hazel finished scooping the last balloon out of the net and released it into the air. She jumped back up and waved once again. A smile took over Sawyer's entire face. He reached out the car window and stretched his arm out as far as he possibly could and waved back at his friend. He had forgotten that his phone was still in his hand when it started to buzz. He checked the screen and saw a picture message from Hazel. It was Hope jumping over Winter. "W + H say they'll miss you, too," Hazel had typed.

Sawyer looked back at the roof and gave Hazel one last wave. *There are a lot of things I am going to miss on my semester away,* he thought. He tapped a button on his phone and was typing as Lorraine started the car engine. She was about to pull back onto the road when a huge white thing swooped right past the windshield.

"Whoa!" Lorraine exclaimed. "What was THAT?"

Sawyer looked out the front window and watched a familiar creature soar across the sky toward CMA. *It couldn't be, could it?* "RUFUS?!"

The bird soared over the roof wall, past the balloons, and landed right next to Hazel. *AWP!* He squawked and fluffed his feathers as if he had never been gone. Before Hazel had time to react, she heard a ping coming from her phone. "Thanks, Hazel," Sawyer had written. "You're the best." Hazel swallowed and gazed at Sawyer's car as it drove down the highway. A few tears had welled up in her eyes, but she blinked them away quickly. She turned back to her feathered friend, who was now waddling over to the rooftop pools. Hazel chuckled and followed the bird. She had a lot to tell him.

Sawyer shifted in his seat and settled back. In a couple of hours he would be on a plane, and before he knew it he'd be on a ship in the middle of the ocean. He gazed at the photo of Hope and Winter on his phone. Sawyer was so proud of Winter. He didn't know if dolphins felt emotions like fear, joy, and sadness. But when Winter sighed or nuzzled Sawyer, it felt like she did. Winter had been through some tough times. She had faced physical loss and the loss

of a great friend. She had suffered through deep sadness and loneliness. But she had figured out that the
hard stuff came along with friendship and joy, too.
That life had all of that in it. When Sawyer told her
that he would come back to see her after his semester
away, he was sure she understood. He remembered
what he told Winter when he was saying good-bye:
When one door closes, another opens. Life is full of
possibilities.

Inspired by a True Story

Mandy was last seen healthy and happy in the Gulf of Mexico.

The team at CMA continues to improve Winter's tail. The black flukes make the tracking of her movements more precise, and improvements in technology continue every day.

Winter and Hope are thriving and have become the best of friends, and can be seen at CMA or online at SeeWinter.com. As CMA continues to grow, the two dolphins remain an inspiration to millions around the world.